The Vampire of Wembley

and Other Tales of Murder, Mystery, and Mayhem

The Vampire of Wembley

And Other Tales of Murder, Mystery, and Mayhem

by Edgar Wallace

Contents

The Vampire of Wembley

THE gentle Tressa was remarkable in one respect: she never found bad people interesting.

When Lady Mary Midston told her about the burglar, Tressa was politely interested but not enthusiastic.

"Daddy was in Paris, otherwise I should have called him when I heard the noise in the hall. He's simply furious with me for not calling Thomas. When I got downstairs there was a light in the drawing-room and a little man was tying up the silver in a tablecloth. I must say, Tressa, that he was awfully decent, and when he told me about his sick wife and his poor little children I hadn't the heart to call any of the staff."

"And you let him go?" said Tressa, coldly for her. "My child, you have a certain duty to society—I suppose you realise that? I know you acted as your own kind little heart dictated, but a burglar is a burglar, no matter what the state of his wife's health—"

"That's what daddy said," remarked Mary complacently.

She was a slim, pretty girl, with flawless colouring and anybody but Mike Long would have spent sleepless nights in the fear of losing her. Mike, for the moment being in the grip of the Wembley Vampire, spent his evenings composing letters breaking off the engagement and his mornings in tearing them up.

"My dear Tressa, you are most original! Of course I let him go! And he was an honest man, apart from his burglaries, for he gave me his address, and when I went—"

"You went to his house?" gasped Tressa.

Mary nodded.

"Of course I went I wanted to know whether his story was true. And, darling, it was! He's got two of the sweetest children, and a wretched, washed-out kind of wife without an 'h' to her name. And I've asked my cousin Arkwright, who's in the City, to find him a job, so that he will never have to go out burgling any more."

Tressa sighed; and then, after a pause:

"Perhaps you're right," she said, "and I am wrong. But I must confess that I do not like the most picturesque of burglars, and he doesn't seem to have been particularly attractive. Bad people do not appeal to me."

Mary said nothing, but thought a great deal, and Tressa, who was something of a thought-reader, smiled and went on:

"Meeting bad people in one's own circle is unavoidable; and besides, there's just a chance that one may be able to switch them on to the right track."

Mary sniffed.

"If you can switch Lila Morestel on to the right track, I shall be both surprised and pleased," she said.

The taunt was not without justification, for Lila had been a constant visitor at the Piccadilly flat in the past few weeks.

"That is one of the things I cannot understand about you, Tressa. Everybody knows about Mrs. Morestel. Why, they took her name off the books of the Jacara Club and they are pretty broad-minded."

"Lila is in trouble and wanted my help," said Tressa shortly.

*

LILA MORESTEL was frequently in trouble: and as frequently, in her helpless, agonised way, appealed for the assistance of her friends. Sometimes the assistance was such that it could not be rendered without damage to the reputation of the helper.

Her history was a curious one. She had been a shop assistant in an Oxford Street establishment, and her beauty attracted the attention of Vivian Morestel. Nobody knew how Vivy earned his living. It was supposed that he sold cars on commission, and that he acted as agent for a firm of bookmakers in various members' enclosures. He had other sources of income, which only the unfortunate young men who accepted invitations to play cards in his flat knew anything about, and they were naturally reticent.

For some inexplicable reason his hectic courtship of Lila culminated within a few weeks of his meeting her in a visit to the Marylebone Registry Office, where they were joined together in the business-like bonds of matrimony.

Lila's social progress was amazing. There were vague stories in circulation of tremendous adventures with wealthy members of the British aristocracy, and the officials of the Royal Courts of Justice could tell of divorce suits begun by Vivy and 'settled out of court' for a consideration. Generally the sum was about £20,000, and Mr. and Mrs. Vivy Morestel grew opulent, bought Flynn Hall at Wembley, and lived there alternately.

Vivy had discovered a method of earning a livelihood more effective than the most cleverly manipulated pack of cards could give him. There were minor scandals within scandals. Big, bluff Scherzo, the maître d'hôtel at the Fourways Club, complained bitterly that he had introduced Lila to a rich Brazilian and that, no sooner had Lila got her landing hooks into his banking account, than she persuaded him to patronise another establishment—a dead loss to Scherzo of £100 a week, for the Brazilian was a liberal spender.

By mutual consent the two young people lived apart, and only met either in consultation, to decide for how much they could bleed Lila's latest friend, or else to cut up the profits over a pleasant dinner. This sounds incredible, but it is true, and the partnership might have continued for a very long time, with profit to both but Vivy made the mistake of falling in love with somebody, and decided on a real divorce.

That is the story of Lila, known to every clubman in London. It is the story behind the dazzling picture of her published in the daily and weekly press. Into the web of Flynn Hall many bloated flies had flown and struggled helplessly, and had been duly blooded. And now the king fly was buzzing nearer and nearer to the viscid threads.

"I can only tell you, Tressa, that if she gets Mike I'll—I'll murder her!"

Tressa laughed softly.

"Mike's much too sensible," she said, conscious of her own hypocrisy, for she had told other women that other men were 'much too sensible,' and had had to watch the ruin of hopes and ambitions that littered the trail where the triumphant Lila had passed.

She decided in this particular case that it would be wise to see Mike himself; but days passed before she met him, and then the opportunity—it was at the opening match at Hurlingham—was not a particularly good one.

Mike listened, obviously ill at ease, whilst Tressa expatiated on the virtues and sweetness of his fiancée.

"Yes, of course, that's all right," he said awkwardly at last. "Mary is a dear—much too good for me, and all that sort of thing. I wouldn't hurt her for the world. But I'm not so sure that our marriage would be the best thing for her in the long run. Honestly, Tressa, I'd give a million pounds if she'd get fed up with me and break it off."

"Why?" asked Tressa.

Mike fumbled with his tie, ran his hand through his fair hair, pulled at his aristocratic nose, and stammered something about incompatability.

"The point is, Tressa," he said at last. "Mary's much too sweet a girl to marry a rough-and-tumble fellow like me. She's unsophisticated, and it would simply hurt me most damnably to upset her. She's a child. I feel that I ought to marry a girl who has—well, suffered—give her a sort of safe harbour after the storm."

"In fact, Lila Morestel," said Tressa brutally, and Mike went very red.

"Well, yes; I'm awfully fond of Lila, and she's had a perfect hell of a time with that awful husband of hers. You've no idea, Tressa, what that girl has suffered."

"I have a pretty shrewd idea, I think," said Tressa drily, and Mike grew a little peevish.

"Of course, if you are one of the people who believe all these awful stories that are told about her, there's no use in continuing the argument," he said. "'Malice loves a shining mark', Tressa, and naturally these beastly women who invent all kinds of stories about the poor girl...."

Tressa realised that this was not the moment to give her views on Lila Morestel and her sufferings. More especially she was embarrassed by the knowledge that she had been the unwilling recipient of that lady's confidence.

When she got home she wrote a little note asking Lila to come and see her, and the next morning came a telephone call from Flynn Hall.

"Is it very important, darling? I'm simply rushed off my feet. I have to see my solicitors today or tomorrow—or perhaps it's next Monday: I'm not quite certain. But anyway, I'm fearfully rushed! You know just how terrible I'm feeling about the whole business."

"Can you come tomorrow?" insisted Tressa, and there came from the other end of the wire a reluctant agreement.

"You know I'm selling Flynn Hall?" she added, just as Tressa thought the conversation was ended and was about to replace the receiver.

*

IT was perfectly true that Lila contemplated the sale of Flynn Hall. She discussed the matter with Vivy, who came to lunch that day, and he completely agreed with her plans. They sat together in the beautiful, panelled library that looked out on a stretch of lawn and a well tended garden. Lila was at her desk, and had before her a neat array of title deeds and accounts; for she was a business woman of extraordinary ability, methodical to a painful degree—it pained Vivy at any rate—even going so far as to keep the records of many strange but thrilling incidents in a steel filing cabinet. Because, as Lila told her husband:

"You never know when these things may be useful."

A cigarette drooped from Vivy's thin lips, his pale blue eyes surveyed the pleasant vista in a melancholy stare, his hands were thrust deep into his pockets, and his shoulders humped—a favourite attitude of his when he found himself in hopeless conflict with his businesslike partner.

"Well, have it your own way, Lila," he said, "only tell me when you've made the decision. I've never known you to be so undecided before. It seems a perfectly easy thing to do: you can bring a petition: I'll not defend it; and that will be the end of it."

She looked at him thoughtfully.

"I'm not sure that is the best way," she meditated. "Mike and I went to the El Moro last night and had a long talk. He's worth three millions, Vivy, but the money is so tied up that I can't see myself handling a great deal of it."

"Here, what do you mean?" asked Vivian, galvanised to activity in his alarm. "You're not going to cry off? I've promised that dear girl—"

"Never mind what you've promised that dear girl," snapped Lila. "And how you can bring yourself to fall in love with her is beyond me. I'm not going to cry off—I want to marry Mike."

"Isn't he engaged or something?" asked Vivy, with a flicker of interest. "I thought he was tied up with Lady Mary Midston— rather a pretty girl, too."

"He's tied up with nobody," said Lila decisively. "He likes her, and I suppose he is sort of engaged to her. I know he's rather worried about breaking it off, but that's nothing. The point is this"—she folded her hands on the desk and looked him straight in the eyes—"will it be the best for me to divorce you or for you to divorce me? If I bring the action, there's nothing in it for either of us, and there's always a chance that he might back out. On the other hand, if you bring the action, Mike's got such a strange sense of honour that he's certain to marry me and, what is more, there would be a settlement."

Now settlements had been the foundation of Lila's fortune and, incidentally, of Vivy's and they were now on ground familiar to both.

"Only this time, of course," Lila went on, "there would be no cut. Whatever I got would be mine, and I think, with a bit of luck, we could induce Mike to pay a hundred thousand pounds out of court. The only thing is that is mustn't be settled on me, otherwise it might affect my marriage settlement."

Vivian was now thoroughly alert, and for an hour they discussed ways and measures. At the end of that time Lila made a neat little memorandum of the arrangement, cursed her husband for his rapacity—he had ultimately accepted an eight per cent commission—and there, so far as the vampires were concerned, the matter was satisfactorily ended.

To Tressa, the next afternoon, she gave her own version of the agreement.

"My dear, the most terrible thing has happened! Vivy is filing a suit for divorce."

Tressa was staggered.

"He is divorcing you?" she said incredulously. "I thought—"

"I know, I know," said Lila, wringing her hands. She was a tall, svelte woman, with a willowy figure, an over-large chin and eyes of melting blue.

"Isn't it too dreadful, Tressa! And after all I have done for him, the sacrifices I have made, after all my subterfuges to keep his name clean!"

"Of course, Mike will defend the action, and you will counterpetition?" said Tressa.

Lila shook her head sadly.

"I could do that, of course," she said mournfully, "but my dear, think of the publicity—I would make any sacrifice for Mike's sake. In fact, I've just seen him and told him so. You can't realise what this means to me, Tressa."

"But," said the incredulous Tressa, "You're not allowing Vivian to bring this action and offering no defence, are you?"

"What can I do?" wailed Lila. "I have to consider Mike. It's the awful publicity of a defended action that I'm thinking about." Tressa frowned.

"Is your husband asking for damages?" she demanded suspiciously.

"I don't know what he's doing. My head is in a perfect whirl, and I'm positively sick with worry and anxiety," said Lila. "Mike has been awfully good about the whole thing. Of course, it's come as a great blow to the poor darling, especially as he is, in a manner of speaking, innocent; and he's threatened to kill Vivy. But he realises that he's been seen about with me so much, and under the circumstances he feels, as I do, that the thing to avoid is publicity—"

"How much is Vivy asking?"

Lila threw out tragic and despairing hands.

"I haven't the slightest idea, darling," she whimpered. "Please don't ask me! The thing is so sordid and horrible that it doesn't bear speaking of."

Mike Long, a very dazed and serious young man, sat down that night and sent a letter which took him two hours to compose; and Mary Midston read it in bed and did not shed a tear. She read it twice, read it again, and then, reaching out of bed, lifted the telephone and called Tressa.

"Have you heard the news?" she asked.

Tressa, who had come in to breakfast early in the expectation of this call, replied cautiously:

"What news is this, Mary?"

"I've had a letter from Mike," said Mary, and her voice was singularly even for one whose engagement had been so unceremoniously broken off. "I won't read it to you, but it's all about my youth and innocence, and the horrible unworthiness of Mike. In fact, Tressa, he's ditched me!"

Tressa winced: she had never taken to the argot of the streets.

"And he's going to marry the Vampire. In fact, Mr. Vampire is bringing an action for divorce, and Mike is the Foolish Third."

There was a long pause.

"What are you going to do?" asked Tressa.

"I'm going to do all that I'm not expected to do," said the cool voice at the other end of the line. "I should be sobbing into my pillow, or writing a tear-stained letter. But, Tressa, I'm not going to allow that poor child—"

"Which poor child?" asked the startled Tressa.

"Mike," was the calm reply. "Do you know anybody who better fills the description? I'm not going to allow him to be ruined by that unspeakable reptile. I'm supposed to be unsophisticated but, Tressa, though I neither dope nor drink, nor indulge in the peculiar pleasures of our mutual friends, I know just enough of the wicked world and its ways to stop this divorce."

"How?" asked Tressa.

"Ha ha!" said the voice, so sardonic that for the second time within twenty-four hours Tressa was staggered.

"I know something about Lila," Mary went on, "and I'm going to learn a little more. Do you remember how she once settled a dispute we had at dinner, as to who won the money when we all went to Ascot with the Gladdings, by producing a four-year-old race-card with all the accounts neatly pencilled on the back?"

"But what on earth has that to do with the divorce?" asked Tressa in amazement.

"We shall see," said Mary, and rang off.

Mike Long was on the point of going out that night when the visitor was announced, and he almost collapsed at the sight of the girl in shimmering blue and white who confronted him in the drawing-room.

"Mary!" he stammered. "My dear, I'm sorry you came. I don't think it's wise of you to distress yourself."

"I'm not distressing myself at all," said Mary. "I thought I would come along and make your mind easy. I'm consoling myself with Social Snaps".

"With what?" gasped Mike.

Had his brutal conduct turned this unfortunate girl's brain?

"You may not have heard of Social Snaps, she said apologetically. "It isn't a very high-class paper—in fact, daddy says that it is a very low- class paper. It has been advertised for sale in the Press for months—you must have read the announcements. I bought it—daddy lent me the money."

"But why in the name of fate do you want to go in for that sort of thing?"

He was so astonished that he forgot the painfulness of the interview.

"You're not a journalist—you can't write—"

"Can't I?" she said darkly. "Oh, can't I!"

He looked at her uncomfortably.

"I'm glad—I mean, I'm glad that you have taken things so well. The whole business is rather awful, isn't it? Vivy is a so-and-so, but I've got to go through with it. You don't know how terrible I'm feeling...."

He babbled further inanities, and she heard him through. Then she made a statement, and he went red and then white.

"You mustn't say that sort of thing about Lila: she's as innocent as a child, and all these stories about her are lies. It is infamous to suggest that she has lived on blackmail—wicked!"

"You must subscribe to my paper, Mike," she said at parting. "Can you drop me at the comer of Russett Street, Lambeth? I saw your car at the door."

"Where!" he squeaked. "Russett Street—why that's one of the lowest neighbourhoods in London!"

"We journalists have to go to strange places," said Mary.

*

IT was on the fourth day of the second week after this interview that Lila stalked tragically into Tressa's room and dropped onto a chair.

"If I could only find the man I'd give him five thousand pounds," she groaned. "The fool didn't trouble to take my jewel case."

"But why should a burglar trouble to rob your library?" asked Tressa, who had read the account of the burglary in the morning newspaper.

"Because—I don't know!" snapped the Vampire. "Oh my God, why did he? Every paper taken from my safe, every letter stolen from my file! He must have spent hours. And there were two of them. The fool of a policeman said that he saw a little man and a woman coming down the drive and got into a car that was waiting on the road."

"Who was the woman?"

Lila could only wave despairing hands.

Tressa was genuinely puzzled for a day or two, and then one morning there came to her breakfast table a small weekly journal. She tore off the wrapper to examine Mary's initial effort as a journalist, and the first thing that caught her eye was a black letter announcement.

In our next issue we shall tell the story of:
The Vampire of Wembley
and publish extracts from correspondence between
this sinister woman, her wretched victims, and her horrible husband.
We shall also give the confessions of a converted burglar who,
owing to the influence exercised by a young and charming society
woman, was induced to return to the paths of virtue.
Order Your Copies Now

And then Tressa understood.

Lila read the marked paragraph sent to her by registered post and also understood.

She got on the telephone to Vivy.

"That Midston girl has got the letters, Vivy. I don't know what you'll do, but I'm going to California till things look brighter. I think that is the only way to stop publication. Oh, yes, Mike has a copy of the worst letters. I called him up a few minutes ago, and his valet told me that he was not at home to me."

The Vampire of Wembley

Halley's Comet, the Cowboy and Lord Dorrington

LORD DORRINGTON was a middle-aged man. He showed no evidence of mental decrepitude, and the alienist who was invited on one occasion to dine with his lordship—the invitation came from anxious relatives, who feared that, unless the poor dear fellow was placed under proper control, he would dissipate the fortunes of the Dorrington family—this alienist wrote so cheery a report upon Dorrington's health that the question of the payment of his fifty-guinea fee was seriously debated. It was felt by a select committee, composed of the beneficiaries under Dorrington's will, that the alienist had not done his duty. They called him (the alienist), disrespectfully, the 'mad doctor', and decided that his report upon Dorrington's sanity was a remarkable proof of the generally-accepted theory that all alienists become mad themselves—in time.

The reason for their fears for Lord Dorrington's reason is understandable. He was an enthusiastic seeker after light. He was a spiritualist, a student of thaumaturgy, theurgy, electro-biology, and something of a Shamanist in an amateur kind of way. He believed that unlikely things happened.

It must be understood that he was, in many ways, a practical man. He once had a butler who neglected the silver horribly. The butler's somewhat ingenious excuse that he also was given to occult studies, and was, moreover, a cadet in the practice of demonology, was received coldly. Further, explained the butler, the silver was cleaned every day, but by night there came a little devil who smeared his dirty paws all over the polished surface of the plate. 'A little devil named 'Erbert, me lord,' said the butler pathetically, 'who cursed me when I was born.'

'You have been reading German fairy tales,' said his lordship, with chilly hauteur, 'and your impudent excuses decide me: I shall not give you a character.'

It was obviously absurd and unthinkable that even a little devil should condescend to consort with a mere butler, and Lord Dorrington very properly resented the assumption of his servant.

Dorrington was a rich man and a shrewd man. The Dorrington belt was the eighth wonder of the world, as any guide-book to the castle will tell you. It was the belt presented by an English king to a lady who was the founder of the family. It was six inches broad, and made of diamonds—not large diamonds, but very saleable diamonds. The Dorrington strong-room was the strongest strong-room in England, for many people desired those gems, the market value being somewhere in the neighbourhood of £80,000.

Lord Dorrington, as I say, was very practical in such matters, and where many a less fanciful man might have contented himself with phylacteries, his lordship, though a student of phylacteries, pinned his faith to doors of chilled steel and Chubb locks.

It would occupy a great deal too much space to give at any length the number of attempts which were made upon those strong-rooms at Dorrington Castle.

There was the still-room maid, who came with forged credentials from an eminent domestic agency, whose box contained diamond drills and a portable axe. There was the groom of the chambers, so suave and polite, with a hundred-pound 'kit' of well-tempered, safe-breaking tools. There was the Swiss valet, who was so very satisfactory until he was discovered one sad night walking cautiously in his stockinged feet in the direction of the strong-room. His explanation that, as a connoisseur of paintings, he desired an uninterrupted study of his lordship's 'Ribera Espanolito' in the east gallery was not accepted by a sceptical bench of magistrates, who gently pointed out that the skeleton keys found in his possession were not consistent with his statement.

These and many others I could name.

Whatever views his relatives might have concerning his mental balance, I am happy to say that in select criminal circles the acumen and intelligence of Lord Dorrington was held in the greatest respect.

'Not that he's so wonderfully clever,' said Billy the Boy (sometimes called Willie the Nut), 'for, in spite of his electric bells and alarms, three men working together could open the safe—only the devil of it is that it's as much as we can do to get one man inside.'

The Vampire of Wembley

His companions in crime—they were dining at Figgioli's, in Conduit Street, and were beautifully arrayed—nodded their heads in approval.

'They tell me,' said Augustus (nobody knew his other name), 'that a New York crowd are thinkin' about—'

'Let 'em think,' said Billy contemptuously. 'If we can't do the job, they can't.'

There was some justification for such arrogance, for Billy the Boy was a master of his craft, and one remarks, with a glow of national pride, that for scientific burglary England's old supremacy stands unassailed.

I record this conversation that you may have a true appreciation of Lord Dorrington's contadictory qualities, and because he occupied a position of some fame a month or so later, and every scrap of information concerning him is of interest. He was, too, something of a biologist, but that has nothing whatever to do with this story.

You may remember that the year 1910 was chiefly remarkable for the visitation of Halley's comet, and for the fact that the world passed through the tail of our celestial visitor. Now, in spite of lucid articles appearing over the signatures of eminent astronomers, and set forth prominently in the popular organs of public opinion, proving beyond doubt that you might take the tail of Halley's comet and fold the whole of it into a grip sack, there were hundreds of thousands of people who shook in their shoes at the mere thought of the phenomenon they were to witness. As one pseudo-scientific writer querulously pointed out, nobody had ever packed the tail into a portmanteau, so that it was ridiculous to say that such a thing could be done without creasing the tail and ruining it beyond repair. But the most important contribution to the literature on the subject was a letter signed 'Dorrington', which appeared in The Times. It began: 'There is something more than a material aspect to the approaching comet...' and went on to deal with the extraordinary happenings which had coincided with its appearance in former years.

For my own part, (concluded Lord Dorrington soberly) I anticipate remarkable results from the visitation. For the first time in the world's history we have the scientific equipment to register and convey simultaneously the observations of psychists the world over....

There were gross and sordid writers in Fleet Street who guffawed loudly on reading this; worse, they wrote sarcastic paragraphs and little poems, and generally shocked the psychic world by their levity.

But their confusion came quickly.

The comet came, growing brighter and brighter nightly, and, as the superb spectacle increased in splendour, the world began to take the comet more and more seriously.

The earth entered the comet's tail on May 18th, and quite a number of people sat up all night destroying so much of their correspondence as, being recovered from the week of the world, might tend to make them look ridiculous.

But nothing happened on the night of the 18th, and the sun rose on the 19th in very much the same way as usual.

The busy world awoke, and went about its work. Factory horns hooted the toiling millions to labour, trim maids knocked at innumerable doors with tea and buttered toast, and the charwoman reigned supreme in the City of London.

At 7.15, PC Albert Parker, of the City Police, came leisurely out of Shoe Lane into Wine Office Court. He turned the corner of the court, and came to a narrow stretch which leads into Fleet Street. On the left is the white-bricked wall of the Daily Telegraph paper store, on the right is the dingy facade of the Press Club. Lying between the Press Club and the far end of the court was the body of a man. 'Lying' is hardly the word, for he sprawled face downward, with arms and legs outstretched in spread-eagle fashion.

PC Parker hastened his steps, and came up to the prostrate figure.

It was clad in the most extraordinary garments. The trousers were of undressed sheepskin, with the woolly side outermost; a dark blue shirt was on his back, and round his neck was a gaudy neckcloth of great size. Under his baggy trousers he wore top-boots, and two large silver spurs stuck up, sparkling in the sunlight. Add to this a broad-brimmed hat, which lay at some distance from the figure, and a huge revolver at his side.

The constable knelt down and felt the man's face; it was quite warm. He turned the figure over on its back. The man was breathing regularly, his heart was strong and normal; he appeared to be in a deep sleep.

PC Parker frowned, and smelt his breath. No, he was not drunk, and the policeman shook the man by the shoulder.

'Come along,' he said sternly; 'you can't sleep here.'

The man drew a long breath, sighed, and opened his eyes, blinking at the light. He stared at the policeman, and the policeman stared at him. The stranger was about thirty years of age; he was unshaven, and his face was covered with a faint coating of white dust.

'Gee!' he said, and sat up, scratching his head. Then he yawned, stretched himself, and rose a little shakily. 'Whar's that all fired hoss of mine?' he demanded sleepily.

'Look here,' said the policeman, 'what's this—a circus performance?'

The stranger stared coolly at the officer of the law.

'Say,' he repeated, 'whar's that old greaser of mine?'

Then he seemed of a sudden to realise that something had happened.

He looked up and down the deserted court curiously. He allowed his eyes to wander along the buildings, then they came back to the policeman with a scared look.

Then he passed his hand over his forehead wearily.

'I was goin' out to brand a steer,' he said, in a dreamy voice, 'an' that old light, she came prancin' over the prairie—she was a sure enough comet's tail, an' she hit me good. Where am I?' he asked suddenly.

'You're in the City of London,' said the police constable; 'and I'm going to take you along to the station.'

The strange sleeper staggered back.

'City of hell!' he roared. 'I'm in Colefax, Texas. Whar's my horse?'

Four policemen, hastily summoned by a shrill whistle, hustled the cowboy—for such he evidently was—to the Bridewell, and two hours later, charged with being 'a suspected person' the man in the sheepskin chapperos came up at Guildhall before the alderman.

That he told the same story, only more coherently, of the 'sure enough comet which came prancing over the plains about Colefax, Tex.,' is evidenced by the fact that at noon there was not a newspaper bill in London which was not screaming the news of the extraordinary occurrence. I give you the headlines of one of the more sedate of the evening newspapers:

AMAZING DISCOVERY IN THE CITY
COWBOY CAUGHT UP BY THE COMET'S TAIL
DEPOSITED IN LONDON
ASTRONOMER-GENERAL SAYS IT IS IMPOSSIBLE.

It was the one great splash of news of the day—nay, it was the most amazing happening of the century. Astronomers became apoplectic in their attempt that the whole thing was impossible. Yet—but let me quote The Evening Advertiser:

...Another extraordinary fact is that when the man was taken to Bridewell his face and hair were covered with thin, white powder. The City surgeon, who was called to examine the man, took the trouble to brush some of this powder off, and submit it to analysis. It proved to be a fine alkaline matter, such as a man might accumulate in a ride across the alkali plains which abound in that part of the world from which the man said he came. Moreover, on being searched, he was found to be in possession of ten five-dollar bills, a Mexican five-dollar piece, some loose American money, and, most remarkable of all, a receipted hotel bill. The bill was for 'one night bed' at Golden South Hotel, in a town in Texas, and was dated May 17th, 1910. There was also a note of some laundry work done on the same date, and some thin hide laces, wrapped up in an American newspaper, which, although the title was undecipherable or torn off, has the date fairly legible, and that date is May 18th.

The Vampire of Wembley

This, and other evidence of the extraordinary character of the visitor, may be found in The Psychical Magazine, if it is not destroyed—but I rather fancy that that particular number of the publication in question has been burnt.

It is no exaggeration to say that England talked of nothing else but 'the man the comet brought', and that there was not a psychical society in the world but hastily assembled to gather data upon the remarkable visitation.

Excitement was at its height, when a new and even more sensational discovery was made.

The particulars may be given in the words of The Sussex Times:

A sensational affair has happened at Eastergate, which has caused great local excitement. It appears that a number of horses from Mr Alfred Knight's training establishment were proceeding along the road in the direction of the downs, when the leading horse, Master Hopmoon, shied at the figure of a man lying by the side of the road. It is by no means a strange thing to observe tramps sleeping out at this time of the year, but the remarkable fact about the present case was that the figure was that of a Chinaman. The boy cantered back to where Mr Knight and his head lad were riding, behind the exercising horses, and informed his master. Mr Knight immediately rode forward and, dismounting, examined the man. Apparently the Chinaman was sleeping. He was dressed in the costume of his country, and Mr Knight informed our representative that the man was evidently one of the labouring class of China.

As might be expected, the newcomer did not speak a word of English. He seemed dazed and terrified, and was with difficulty persuaded to accompany Mr Knight to the Eastergate Drill Hall, where temporary accommodation was found for him until the police were communicated with. Much greater difficulty was found in persuading him to get into the train at Barnham Junction, to accompany the police to Arundel. The man was in a condition of abject fright, jabbering and gesticulating as though he had never seen a railway train in his life. Fortunately, there lives in Arundel the Rev J. Wiggs, who has, until recently, been a missionary in China, and the rev. gentleman had no difficulty in conversing with the Celestial.

So much for The Sussex Times. It was after that memorable conversation with the Rev J. Wiggs that the story of the Chinaman acquired a larger value. No man in England read that interview with greater interest than Lord Dorrington. He read it in the The Morning News, and straightway took a train for London, and thence to Arundel.

'It is quite true, my lord,' said the Rev J. Wiggs, a little bewildered by the extraordinary experience of the previous day. 'I saw him as soon as he arrived. He is a Chinaman from the province of Yste-Yang; so far as I can make out he is a boatman. His story is so remarkable that my head whirls with it.'

'What is it?' demanded Lord Dorrington, not unprepared for the answer.

'Virtually he tells the same story as was told by the cowboy who was, as your lordship may know, discovered two days ago in the City of London.'

Lord Dorrington nodded.

'He says,' continued the returned missionary, 'that in the cool of the morning he was walking through a rice-field, in the direction of the village of Lung-tsi-lang, where he had made an appointment to meet a moneylender, who wished to marry his daughter. He had noticed, with fear, the apparition of the comet, and as he walked he faced that portion of the sky where the tail of the comet showed dimly. If anything, as he says, the comet was less brilliant than it had been. But on the horizon he observed a curious light. According to his account, it was a 'great wall of silver dust', which rose higher and higher, and became more and more brilliant, until, terrified by the apparition and by the almost blinding dazzle of the vision, he stopped, covering his face with his hands. He heard a whistling roar and lost consciousness, and the next thing that he knew was that he was lying on a soft, grass bank, and a foreign devil was talking to him in a strange tongue.'

Later, Dorrington saw the Chinaman, very sullen, and showing as much evidence of his fear as his natural imperturbability of countenance allowed.

Lord Dorrington returned to London to find a small crowd of reporters awaiting him at Victoria, to face innumerable cameras, and to answer a hundred questions.

'No,' he said, shaking his head, when questioned by the special representative of The Morning News, 'I am not in a position to give my theories as to the remarkable happenings of the past two days. I have my own ideas concerning them, but they are not sufficiently definite to give to the world. I intend bringing both men to Dorrington Castle, and, through an interpreter as far as the Chinaman is concerned, collect as much data as possible before these victims of astral phenomena are returned to their homes.'

'Do you think that these comet translations have occurred elsewhere?' demanded the reporter.

'I do,' replied his lordship. 'In a day or so, in a few hours perhaps, we shall have further manifestations of the comet's power.'

The newspapers had, by this time, reversed their attitude of amused scepticism, and awarded Lord Dorrington's statement the dignity of leaded type.

His prophecy, and the story of its fulfilment, appeared side by side, for, whilst his lordship had stood in the centre of the interrogating pressmen, the third, and, so far as can be ascertained, the last of the strange visitations, came.

The third was even more dramatic in its circumstances than were the others.

Dorrington had arrived at Victoria at 10 o'clock on the night of the 20th, which fell on a Saturday, and whilst he was giving his views on the phenomena with which all England was ringing, a curious scene was being enacted in one of the theatres.

The curtain had just gone up for the second act of Our Miss Gibbs, at the Gaiety, and the stage was filled with beautiful women, picturesquely grouped, when there entered from one of the wings a figure which brought the play to an immediate standstill, which left the very conductor petrified with upraised baton.

The figure was that of a man, of medium height and enormously stout. He was in evening dress, stained and dusty. His shirt front, in which glittered a huge diamond, was crumpled and grimy, and as he came waddling down the stage, rubbing his eyes and yawning, the immaculate chorus fell back on either side.

He looked around with a puzzled frown, and then addressed a question to the actor nearest to him.

'Señor,' said he, in the dialect of the Estremadura, 'will you, in the names of the blessed saints, inform me where I am?'

The actor, who did not understand a word of Spanish, shook his head, and glanced appealingly to the wings, and the curtain was rung down amidst some excitement.

This, indeed, was the third visitant!

José Sebastian Lopez, to give him the name by which he described himself, was a Brazilian, on a holiday visit to Spain. His story, inscribed in Lord Dorrington's neat handwriting, is not the least interesting of the memoranda on the men who were hit by the comet:

I am (says this document) a native of Brazil, although I cannot tell you what part of Brazil, for the time being, for I seem to have lost my memory. I arrived in Madrid on the night of the 16th, and stayed at the Hotel de Paris, on the Puerta del Sol. On the 17th, I believe, though I am not certain in my mind, I saw a man with whom I had some business relations. Who he was, or what was the nature of his business, I forget, but probably, when my head is less clouded, I shall recall the matter. The next day I spent in walking about Madrid. I have a dim idea that I went to the Prado, and that I spent some time admiring the old Spanish masters. In the evening I know that I dressed for dinner, and, the evening being a warm one, I went out without my overcoat, to the Casino. I left the Casino late. It must have been in the early hours of the morning but there were a number of people about and most of the cafés were open. I went up to my room and sat by the open window, smoking a cigar. It was then that over the houses, to the west side of the Puerta del Sol, I noticed a strange white light in the sky, resembling a pillar of white fire, which expanded in breadth visibly as I watched it. It grew broader and broader, and I pinched myself, thinking I must be dreaming. I sat with open mouth, paralysed, and the light grew fiercer and fiercer, till I felt it envelop me. I had no sensation of warmth, only a strange feeling of lightness, as though I could step through the window into the street below without hurt—and that was all I remember. When I awoke I found myself in a strange building. There was above me a skylight, which was open, and through which I must have fallen. I knew that I was in a theatre, for the curtain was raised, and the seats were all shrouded in holland, but I had no feeling of curiosity. All I wanted to do was sleep, sleep, sleep. I climbed over the orchestra on to the stage and wandered around, looking for a place in which to lie, for I was like a man drunk with sleep.

*

Lord Dorrington steadfastly refused to receive any reporters, although some of the best men journeyed down to High Dorrington to secure his views.

'The only thing I can say is this,' said his lordship to a select deputation, whose persistence had secured for themselves a short interview. 'I have, as you know, the three men here at Dorrington Castle. We are, through the instrumentality of interpreters, collecting and comparing everything they say bearing upon their transmigration. I can tell you this much, that their stories tally in every respect, but the full account of my investigations will be published at a very early date. The cowboy seems to have the most vivid recollection of all that happened, and I am certain that we have at last a manifestation of an occult mystery which will convince the most sceptical.'

Saying this, his lordship ushered the Pressmen from the room, and returned to his strange investigations.

We have not, unfortunately, the minutes of that inquisition, although it has been stated on most reliable authority that they covered reams of foolscap. We may guess that an irritated cowboy, a wondering but impassive Chinaman, and a most voluble gentleman from Mexico sat and suffered as Lord Dorrington, with the cold persistence of the enthusiast, extracted from them the particulars of their varying sensations.

It was the night of the reporters' visit that the fourth and the most inexplicable of the comet's vagaries was recorded. The three men, after a lengthy examination, had retired to their separate bedrooms, and Lord

Dorrington sat alone in his study, revising the notes he had made.

Engrossed in his labours, he did not regard time, and time, utterly independent of Lord Dorrington's patronage, moved ruthlessly forward.

Looking up, in a passionate attempt to find a synonym for 'extraordinary' and 'remarkable', his lordship was astounded to observe that the hands of the clock pointed to half-past two.

He put away his papers, locked them in his desk, lit his bedroom candle, and extinguished the light in the study. Then he made his way along the silent hall toward the big stairway that led to his sleeping suite.

Then, of a sudden, when he was half-way along the broad passage, there came a blinding white flash of flame. It leapt to him, and, as he staggered back, something struck him on the head, and he went to the floor like a log.

Some say that he was stunned, but others aver that it was blue funk that kept his lordship lying on the floor of the hall until an early-rising servant discovered him, and assisted him back to the study.

His first act—and here he showed the soul of the true scientist—was to send for the three men to compare their sensations with his.

There came no answer to the knockings of Lord Dorrington's hired servants. An examination of the rooms led to the discovery that the men were gone. Their beds had not been slept in; there was no sign of their presence.

Lord Dorrington stood before the door of the cowboy's room, a water compress about his head, wrapped in deep thought. The tremendous character of the new phenomenon impressed even him.

He returned to his study, and sent thirty-six telegrams to thirty-six different newspapers, but the wire was in every case the same.

THREE ASTRAL VISITORS AGAIN TRANSMIGRATED.
I MYSELF HAVE EXPERIENCED POWER OF COMET.
SEND REPORTER.—DORRINGTON.

Long before the reporters could possibly respond to the invitation, a tall, clean-shaven man, with bushy eyebrows, came flying up to the great door of the Dorrington demesne, and demanded imperiously to see his lordship.

He spoke with a strong American accent, and, when ushered into Dorrington's presence, nodded curtly.

'You have come,' began my lord, 'to ask about the men—'

'One was a Chink,' interrupted the other rudely, 'one a Spanish fellow, one a tough from our side, I think?'

'That is so,' said Lord Dorrington gravely, 'but a phenomenon which—'

'Phenomenon nothing,' said the brusque stranger. 'They are the Denver three—the cleverest devils that ever held up a bank. Where are they?'

'Gone,' said his lordship, staring at the man.

'Gone!' roared the other. 'Oh, steaming Hades! Gone! See here,' he went on rapidly, 'I'm Torken, of Pinkerton's. I've got a warrant for the lot; they're bank robbers. We've been after them for a year. They're the people who impersonated the Chinese delegation last fall, and got away with the British ambassador's jewels—'

'Jewels?' repeated his lordship faintly.

'Jewels,' said the vigorous American.

Lord Dorrington, supported on the arm of the detective, led the way to the strongest strong-room in England.

Outwardly it appeared as though nothing unusual had occurred, but when his lordship had inserted his key he found the operation was unnecessary, for the door was unlocked and the Dorrington belt was gone.

The Forest of Happy Thoughts

BAILMAN made things snug for the night in his own characteristic fashion: walked round the tent; saw to the guide ropes; put his lantern over the strands of barbed-wire pegged firmly into the ground; carefully inspected his mosquito-net for signs of a stray musca; then turned his attention to the boys. They were squatting round their fire—a voluble, light-hearted assembly.

"Hast night your noise disturbed me," he said, as he passed them. "To-night, when the lo-koli sounds, you will sleep, and, if I be awakened, I will come with my whip, and you will feel great shame."

He spoke in the sonorous tongue of the Bo-mongo people, and, despite the awfulness of his threat, a titter of amusement ran round the circle. Bailman himself grinned into the darkness as he made his way down to the river, not that he would hesitate to use his chicotte upon a disobedient servant. He had too full an acquaintance with the Congo folk to be overmuch exercised at the necessity for employing the stick; but he grinned because twelve months in the wilds had made him half a savage, and he appreciated the humours of pain.

By the river side the little steamer was moored. There was a tiny bay here, and the swift currents of the river were broken to a gentle flow; none the less, he inspected the shore-ends of the wire hawsers before he crossed the narrow plank that led to the deck of the Zaire. The wood was stacked on the deck, ready for tomorrow's run. The new water-gauge had been put in by N'kema, the engineer, as he had ordered; the engines had been cleaned, and Bailman nodded approvingly. He stepped lightly over two or three sleeping forms curled up on the deck, and gained the shore. "Now I think I'll turn in," he muttered, and looked at his watch. It was nine o'clock. He stood for a moment on the crest of the steep bank, and stared back across the river. The night was black; but he saw the outlines of the forest on the other side. He saw the jewelled sky, and the pale reflection of stars in the water. Then he went to his tent, and leisurely got into his pyjamas. He jerked two tabloids from a tiny bottle, swallowed them, drank a glass of water, and thrust his head through the tent opening. "Ho, Sokani!" he called, speaking in the vernacular, "let the lo-koli sound!"

He went to bed.

He heard the rustle of men moving, the gurgles of laughter as his threat was repeated, and then the penetrating rattle of sticks on the native drum—a hollow tree trunk. Fiercely it beat—furiously, breathlessly, with now and then a deeper note as the drummer, using all his art, sent the message of sleep to the camp.

In one wild crescendo the lo-koli ceased, and Bailman turned with a sigh of content and closed his eyes... he sat up suddenly. He must have dozed; but he was wide awake now.

He listened, then slipped out of bed, pulling on his mosquito boots. Into the darkness of the night he stepped, and found N'kema, the engineer, waiting.

"You heard, master?" said the native.

"I heard," said Bailman with a puzzled face, "yet we are nowhere near a village."

He listened.

From the night came a hundred whispering noises, but above all these, unmistakable, the faint clatter of an answering drum. The white man frowned in his perplexity. "No village is nearer than the Bongindanga," he muttered, "not even a fishing village; the woods are deserted—"

The native held up a warning finger, and bent his head, listening. He was reading the message that the drum sent. Bailman waited; he knew the wonderful fact of this native telegraph, how it sent news through the trackless wilds. He could not understand it, no European could, but he had respect for its mystery.

"A white man is here," read the native; "he has the sickness."

"A white man!"

In the darkness Bailman's eyebrows rose incredulously.

"He is a foolish one," N'kema read; "he sits in the Forest of Happy Thoughts and will not move."

Bailman clicked his lips impatiently. "No white man would sit in the Forest of Happy Thoughts," he said, half to himself, "unless he were mad."

But the distant drum monotonously repeated the outrageous news. Here, indeed, in the heart of that loveliest glade in all Africa, encamped in the very centre of the Green Path of Death, was a white man, a sick white man... in the Forest of Happy Thoughts... a sick white man....

So the drum went on and on, till Bailman, rousing his own lo-koli man, sent an answer crashing along the river, and began to dress hurriedly.

In the forest lay a very sick man. He had chosen the site for the camp himself. It was in a clearing, near a little creek that wound between high elephant-grass to the river. Mainward chose it, just before the sickness came, because it was pretty. This was altogether an inadequate reason, but Mainward was a sentimentalist, and his life was a long record of choosing pretty camping places, irrespective of danger. "He was," said a newspaper, commenting on the crowning disaster which sent him a fugitive from justice to the wild lands of Africa, "overburdened with imagination." Mainward was cursed with ill-timed confidence; this was one of the reasons he chose to linger in that deadly strip of the Ituri which is clumsily named by the natives "The Lands-where-all-bad-thoughts-become-good-thoughts," and poetically adapted by explorers, and daring traders, as "The Forest of Happy Dreams." Over-confidence had generally been Mainward's undoing—over-confidence in the ability of his horses to win races; over-confidence in his own ability to secure money to hide his defalcations—he was a director of the Welshire County Bank once—over confidence in securing the love of a woman who, when the crash came, looked at him blankly and said she was sorry, but she had had no idea that he felt towards her like that....

Now Mainward lifted his aching head from the pillow and cursed aloud at the din. He was endowed with the smattering of pigeon-English which a man may acquire from a three months' sojourn, divided between Sierra Leone and Grand Bassam.

"Why for they make 'em cursed noise, eh?" he fretted. "You plenty fool-man, Abiboo."

"Si, senor," agreed the Kano boy calmly.

"Stop it, d'ye hear; stop it!" raved the man on the tumbled bed; "this noise is driving me mad—tell them to stop the drum."

The lo-koli stopped of its own accord, for the listeners in the sick man's camp had heard the faint answer from Bailman's.

"Come here, Abiboo—I want some milk: open a fresh tin; and tell the cook I want some soup, too."

The servant left him muttering and tossing from side to side on the creaking camp bedstead. Mainward had many things to think about. It was strange how they all clamoured for immediate attention; strange how they elbowed and fought one another in their noisy claims to his notice. Of course there was the bankruptcy and the discovery at the bank—it was very decent of that inspector fellow to give him the tip to clear out—and Ethel, and the horses, and—and...

The Valley of Happy Dreams! That would make a good story if Mainward could write, only, unfortunately, he could not write. He could sign things, sign his name "Three months after date pay to the order of—" he could sign other people's names... he groaned and winced at the thought.

But here was a forest where bad thoughts became good, and, God knows, his mind was ill-furnished. He wanted peace and sleep and happiness—he greatly desired happiness. Now suppose "Fairy Lane" had won the Wokingham Stakes? It did not, of course (he winced again at the bad memory), but suppose it had? Suppose he could have found a friend who would have lent him £16,000, or even if Ethel....

"Master," said Abiboo's voice "dem puck-a-puck, him lib for come."

"Eh, what's that?"

Mainward turned almost savagely on the man.

"Puck-a-puck—you hear 'um?"

But the sick man could not hear the smack of the Zaire's stern wheel, as the little boat breasted the downward rush of the river; he was surprised to see that it was dawn, and grudgingly admitted to himself that he had slept. He closed his eyes again and had a strange dream. The principal figure was a tall, tanned, clean-shaven man in a white helmet, who wore a dingy yellow overcoat over his pyjamas.

"How are you feeling?" said the stranger.

"Rotten bad," growled Mainward, "especially about Ethel; don't you think it was pretty low down of her to lead me on to believe that she was awfully fond of me, and then at the last minute to chuck me?"

"Shocking," said the strange white man gravely; "but put her out of your mind just now: she isn't worth troubling about What do you say to this?"

He held up a small greenish pellet between his forefinger and thumb, and Mainward laughed weakly.

"Oh, rot!" he chuckled faintly, "you're one of those Forest of the Happy Dreams johnnies; what's that? a love philter?" He was hysterically amused at the witticism.

Bailman nodded.

"Love or life, it's all one," he said, but apparently unamused, "swallow it."

Mainward giggled and obeyed.

"And now," said the stranger—this was six hours later—"the best thing you can do is to let my boys put you on my steamer and take you down river."

Mainward shook his head. He had awakened irritable and lamentably weak. "My dear chap, it's awfully kind of you to have come—by the way, I suppose you are a doctor?"

Bailman shook his head.

"On the contrary, I am a journalist," he said flippantly, "I'm Bailman, the special correspondent, of The Megaphone. I've been doing atrocities for a year—you know the stuff that is associated with the Congo—but you were saying?"

"I want to stay here—it's devilish pretty."

"Devilish is the very adjective I should have used—my dear man, this is the plague spot of the Congo; it's the home of every death-dealing fly and bug in Congo Land."

He waved his hand to the glorious vista of fresh green glades, of gorgeous creepers that hung their garlands from tree to tree.

"Look at the grass," he said; "it's homeland grass—that's the seductive part of it; I nearly camped here myself—come my friend, let me take you to my camp."

Mainward shook his head obstinately.

"I'm obliged, but I'll stay here for a day or so. I want to try the supernatural effects of this pleasant place," he said with a little smile. "I've got so many thoughts that need treatment."

"Look here," said Bailman roughly, "you know jolly well how this forest got its name; it is called Happy Dreams because it's impregnated with fever, and with every disease from beri-beri to sleeping sickness. You don't wake from the dreams that you dream here. Man, I know this country, and you're a new comer; you've trekked here because you wanted to get away from life and start all over again."

"I beg your pardon." Mainward's face flushed and he spoke a little stiffly.

"Oh, I know all about you—didn't I tell you I was a journalist? I was in England when things were going rocky with you, and I've read the rest in the papers I get from time to time. But all that is nothing to do with me. I'm here to help you to start fair. If you had wanted to commit suicide, why come to Africa to do it? Be sensible and shift your camp; I'll send my steamer back for your men—will you come?"

"No," said Mainward sulkily. "I don't want to, I'm not keen; besides, I'm not fit to travel."

Here was an argument which Bailman could not answer. He was none too sure upon that point himself, and he hesitated before he spoke again.

"Very well," he said at length, "suppose you stay another day to give you a chance to pull yourself together. I'll come along to-morrow with a tip top invalid chair for you—is it a bet?"

Mainward held out his shaking hand, and the ghost of a smile puckered the corners of his eyes. "It's a bet," he said.

He watched the journalist walk through the camp, speaking to one man after another in a strange tongue. A singular, masterful man this, thought Mainward. Would he have mastered Ethel? He watched the stranger with curious eyes, and noted how his own lazy devils of carriers jumped at his word....

"Good-night," said Bailman's voice, and Mainward looked up. "You must take another of these pellets, and tomorrow you'll be as fit as a donkey-engine. I've got to get back to my camp tonight, or I shall find half my stores stolen in the morning; but if you'd rather I stopped?"

"No, no," replied the other hastily. He wanted to be alone. He had lots of matters to settle with himself. There was the question of Ethel, for instance.

"You won't forget to take the tabloid?"

"No. I say, I'm awfully obliged to you for coming. You've been a good white citizen."

Bailman smiled. "Don't talk nonsense," he said, good-humouredly. "This is all brotherly love. White to white, and kin to kin, don't you know? We're all alone here, and there isn't a man of our colour within five hundred miles. Goodnight, and please take the tabloid—"

Mainward lay listening to the noise of the departure. He thought he heard a little bell tingle. That must be for the engines. Then he heard the puck-a-puck of the wheel—so that was how the steamer got its name.

Abiboo came with some milk. "You take um medicine, master?" he inquired.

"I take um," murmured Mainward; but the green tabloid was underneath his pillow.

Then there began to steal over him a curious sensation of content. He did not analyse it down to its first cause. He had had sufficient introspective exercise for one day. It came to him as a pleasing shock to realise that he was happy.

He opened his eyes and looked round. His bed was laid in the open, and he drew aside the curtains of his net to get a better view.

A little man was walking briskly toward him along the velvet stretch of grass that sloped down from the glade, and Mainward whistled.

"Atty," he gasped. "By all that's wonderful."

Atty, indeed, it was: the same wizened Atty as of yore; but no longer pulling the long face to which Mainward had been accustomed. The little man was in his white riding-breeches, his diminutive top-boots were splashed with mud, and on the crimson of his silk jacket there was evidence of a hard race. He touched his cap jerkily with his whip, and shifted the burden of the racing saddle he carried to his other arm,

"Why, Atty," said Mainward, with a smile, "what on earth are you doing here?"

"It's a short way to the jockeys' room, sir," said the little man. "I've just weighed in. I thought the Fairy would do it, sir, and she did."

Mainward nodded wisely. "I knew she would too," he said. "Did she give you a smooth ride?"

The jockey grinned again. "She never does that," he said, "but she ran gamely enough. Coming up out of the Dip, she hung a little, but I showed her the whip, and she came on as straight as a die. I thought once The Stalk would beat us—I got shut in, but I pulled her round, and we were never in difficulties. I could have won by ten lengths," said Atty.

"You could have won by ten lengths," repeated Mainward in wonder. "Well, you've done me a good turn, Atty. This win will get me out of one of the biggest holes that ever a reckless man tumbled into—I shall not forget you, Atty."

"I'm sure you won't, sir," said the little jockey gratefully; "if you'll excuse me now, sir?"

Mainward nodded and watched him as he moved quickly through the trees.

There were several figures in the glade now, and Mainward looked down ruefully at his soiled duck suit. "What an ass I was to come like this," he muttered in his annoyance. "I might have known that I should have met all these people."

There was one he did not wish to see; and as soon as he sighted Venn, with his shy eyes and his big nose, Mainward endeavoured to slip back out of observation. But Venn saw him, and came tumbling through the trees, with his big flabby hand extended and his dull eyes aglow,

"Hullo, hullo!" he grinned, "been looking for you."

Mainward muttered some inconsequent reply. "Rum place to find you, eh?" Venn removed his shining silk hat and mopped his brow with an awesome silk handkerchief.

"But look here, old feller—about that money."

"Don't worry, my dear man," Mainward interposed easily. "I can pay you now."

"That ain't what I mean," said the other impetuously; "a few hundred more or less docs not count. But you wanted a big sum—

"And you told me you'd see me—"

"I know, I know," Venn put in hastily; but that was before Kaffirs started jumpin'. Old feller, you can have it!"

He said this with grotesque emphasis, standing with his legs wide apart, his hat perched on the back of his head, his plump hands dramatically outstretched, and Mainward laughed outright.

"Sixteen thousand?" he asked.

"Or twenty," said the other impressively. "I want to show you—"

Somebody called him, and with a hurried apology he went blundering up the green slope, stopping and turning back to indulge in a little dumb show illustrative of his confidence in Mainward and his willingness to oblige.

Mainward was laughing, a low, gurgling laugh of pure enjoyment. Venn of all people! Venn, with his cursed questions and talk of securities. Well! well! Then his merriment ceased, and he winced again, and his heart beat faster and faster, and a curious weakness came over him.

How splendidly cool she looked.

She walked in the clearing, a white, slim figure: he heard the swish of her skirt as she came through the long grass... white, with a green belt all encrusted with dull gold embroidery. He took in every detail hungrily—the dangling gold ornaments that hung from her belt, the lace collar at her throat, the....

She did not hurry to him: that was not her way.

But her eyes dawned a gradual tenderness—those dear eyes that dropped before his shyly.

"Ethel!" he whispered, and dared to take her hand.

"Aren't you wonderfully surprised?" she said.

"Ethel! here!"

"I—I had to come."

She would not look at him, but he saw the pink in her cheek and heard the faltering voice with a wild hope. "I behaved so badly dear—so very badly."

She hung her head.

"Dear! dear!" he muttered, and groped toward her like a blind man.

She was in his arms, crushed against his breast, the perfume of her presence in his brain.

"I had to come to you—" Her hot cheek was against his. "I love you so."

"Me—love me? Do you mean it?" He was tremulous with happiness, and his voice broke—"dearest."

Her face was upturned to his, her lips so near; he felt her heart beating as furiously as his own. He kissed her—her lips, her eyes, her dear hair....

"O God, I'm happy," he sobbed, "so—so happy...."

Bail man sprang ashore just as the sun was rising, and came thoughtfully through the undergrowth to the camp. Abiboo, squatting by the curtained bed, did not rise. Bailman walked to the bed, pulled aside the mosquito netting and bent over the man who lay there.

Then he drew the curtains again, lit his pipe slowly, and looked down at Abiboo.

"When did he die?" he asked.

"In the dark of the morning, master," said the native.

Bailman nodded slowly. "Why did you not send for me?"

For a moment the squatting figure made no reply, then he rose and stretched himself.

"Master," he said, speaking in Swaheli—that is a language which allows of nice distinctions—"this white man was happy; he walked in the Forest of Happy Thoughts: why should I call him back to a land where there was neither sunshine nor happiness, but only night and the pain of sickness?"

"You're a philosopher," said Bailman irritably.

"I am a follower of the Prophet," said Abiboo, the Kano boy; "and all things are according to God's wisdom."

A Raid on a Gambling Hell

I HAVE had to deal with all classes of society, high and low, rich and poor, and number amongst clients several millionaires, crooks, peers and peeresses, and servant girls. It is my boast that nothing surprises me, yet I must confess feeling a mild tinge of excitement at receiving, on the letter-head of the Ministry of the Interior, a request that I would call at eleven o'clock upon

Mr. George Tresham, the Minister in question.

The Right Honourable George Tresham was a name to conjure with on the day I received that summons. A comparatively young man who had won his way to the foremost Cabinet rank by sheer ability and courage, he had as solid a following as any Minister in the House.

'I have sent for you, Dixon,' he said, 'on a very delicate private matter. A matter,' he went on, 'which affects my personal honour—indeed, affects my whole future career.'

Motioning me to a chair, he began the narrative which is set down below. Of course, I am not giving the real names of persons and places.

George Tresham, in addition to being a popular statesman, was something of a man about town. He had a host of friends, mostly younger than himself, and his interest in the theatre had extended to the writing of a four-act drama, which had been produced with moderate success in the West End. It was during his brief incursion into the realms of dramatic authorship that he made the acquaintance of Bart Philipson—the Honourable Bartholomew Philipson—who, at the time this narrative was told me, had succeeded to his father's very small and very heavily encumbered estate as Lord Colesun.

Bart Philipson, as he was then, had an interest in the theatre wherein Mr. Tresham's play was produced.

The two became fast friends, for George Tresham was a large-hearted, lovable soul, who was attracted rather than repelled by the other's cynicism and worldliness. Tresham was, of course, enormously wealthy.

The two friends were talking at their club one night, and the conversation drifted round to gambling hells. Bart gave a very vivid word-picture of one he had visited in London, and Tresham expressed his surprise that such places existed, and also asked his friend to take him to see one some night.

About a month later, on a Thursday evening, when Tresham had finished his solitary dinner, the telephone bell rang, and his butler told him that Lord Colesun was on the telephone.

'I say,' said Bart's voice, 'are you still keen on seeing one of those places we were speaking about the other night?'

'Rather!' said Tresham, who was bored, and welcomed any diversion.

'Well, there's a new place opened in Montacute Square,' said Bart's voice. 'I don't know very much about it, except that I've got the password and the right of entrée for a friend. I am told it is unique in many respects.'

'All right. I'll come along.'

Tresham ordered his car, picked up Bart, and dismissed the car at the corner of Montacute Square. The two walked on. It was a foggy night, but Bart knew the way.

'Here we are,' he said, and, ascending a short flight of broad steps, he knocked in a peculiar manner on the door.

It was opened by a servant in quiet livery, and after a glance at Bart the two were passed into a hall which was dimly lighted and escorted up a stairway to a landing above. A pair of folding doors confronted them. On this the servant knocked. The door opened a few inches, and a keen eye scrutinised the pair.

'All right; come in, gentlemen,' said the owner of the eye, and they were admitted into a large saloon, blazing with light and richly furnished.

But it was not the appointments which made Tresham stare. It was not even the green table in the centre of the room, around which a dozen men were playing. It was the other questionable occupants. Men and women, the latter in wildly extravagant costumes, were sitting at little tables, taking no notice of the players. They all had the appearance of being under the influence of drink, and very far under at that.

'How perfectly beastly!' Tresham said. 'A perfect saturnalia! Let us get out of this, Bart.'

'I quite agree,' said the phlegmatic Lord Colesun. He was turning to the door, when it burst open, and a wild-eyed servant dashed in.

'The police! The police!' he gasped, and had hardly got the words out of his mouth when two or three policemen burst into the room after an inspector, and were followed by a dozen men in plain clothes. Immediately began a stampede, a kicking over of tables, a screaming of women, a shouting of men. Somebody cried, 'Put out the lights.' One man attempted to unshutter the window, and was pulled back by a constable, and in the end the inspector made his voice heard.

'Ladies and gentlemen,' he said, 'you will all consider yourselves under arrest. I shall take you to Bow Street Police Station.'

'My God! What shall I do?' said Tresham. 'It is ruin, Bart.'

'Keep quiet,' said Bart in a low voice. 'I'll see what I can do.'

He went across to the inspector, and at first the officer would have nothing to say to him. Then Bart said something in a low voice, and the two men stepped aside into a corner of the room, and for a few moments conversed together. Presently Bart strode back to Tresham.

'A policeman will take us out of the door,' he said. 'I've squared him.'

A constable approached and the two men were pushed unceremoniously on to the hall landing and escorted down the stairs.

'All right,' said Bart to the constable and slipped something into his hand.

'Hold hard, sir,' said the policeman, 'I seem to know that gentleman's face.'

'Never mind what you know,' said Bart.

'It's all right, sir. I hope there's no offence,' said the policeman, 'but if that isn't Mr. Tresham, I'm a Dutchman.'

Tresham looked at the man, but could not see his face. He noted, however, that one of his front teeth was broken. In a few moments they were out in the street, Bart cursing himself for having led his friend into such a mess. Tresham stopped him.

'Don't be a fool, Bart,' he said, 'it was my own stupid curiosity which is entirely responsible. What did you say to the inspector fellow?'

'I said a thousand pounds,' said Bart briefly, 'It was the only argument I could think of.'

'Of course I'll pay that,' said Tresham. 'In fact, it's cheap at the price. What about that infernal policeman? Do you think he'll talk?'

'I'll have to go back and see him,' said Bart. 'Otherwise, I don't think there's anybody there who recognised you, not even the inspector.'

George Tresham got home at 11.30, spent a restless night, and when, passing along Whitehall the next afternoon, he saw on the newspaper

The Vampire of Wembley

placards the announcement of a gambling raid, his heart beat faster. Fortunately it was scrappy, merely mentioning the fact that a raid had been made on a house in Montacute Square, that a certain number of people had been arrested, the proprietor had been fined and imprisoned, and that two servants who assisted in the conduct of the house had also been sent to prison. There was no mention of the unpleasant things he had seen; and that afternoon, when Bart came by appointment, the reason was explained.

'I saw the inspector again this morning,' he said, 'and I asked him to keep that part of it quiet, in case it ever came out that I was there. But I'm afraid we're going to have trouble with the policeman,' he went on, shaking his head. 'He's a man named Bowker, a shrewd and unscrupulous fellow, who has been in trouble before, and apparently has already announced his intention of resigning from the force to live upon a private income.'

'What does he mean by that?'

'He means you are the private income, I am afraid.' said Bart grimly.

'Blackmail?' demanded Tresham.

'That's what it amounts to,' said Bart.

'This is dreadful,' said Tresham with a despairing gesture. 'Have you seen this policeman?'

'That's what it amounts to,' said Bart.

'I've just come from him,' said Bart. 'I've found his address—he lives in Bayswater—and made a call. As I feared, he intends making us pay.'

'Did he mention a figure?'

'He did,' said Bart. 'He asked for fifty thousand pounds!'

'Fifty thousand pounds!' Even Tresham was startled.

'Seventy really,' said Bart. 'Fifty from you and twenty from me. Heaven knows where I'm going to get my twenty from.'

Tresham thought for a while.

'When does he want his answer?' he demanded.

'Tomorrow evening at the latest,' said Lord Colesun. 'I have an appointment to meet him on Hammersmith Broadway.'

It was after his friend's departure that Mr. Tresham sat down and wrote the letter that brought me to his study.

I listened in silence and sympathy to the narrative.

'Have you told Lord Colesun that you have sent for me?' I asked.

He shook his head.

'No,' he replied; 'but, of course, I shall tell him.'

'I would rather you didn't,' said I. 'I prefer working under one pair of eyes and with only one set of theories to combat.'

'Namely, mine?' he smiled faintly.

'Namely, yours, sir,' I said. 'You can afford to pay fifty thousand pounds, although I don't suppose anybody can afford to part with such an enormous sum. But Lord Colesun—is it humanly possible that he can pay?'

The Minister shook his head.

'Did he give you the address of the policeman?' I asked.

'No; it is somewhere in Bayswater, but he is meeting him tonight at Hammersmith. You will have to work with Lord Colesun, because he knows the man, and will be able to introduce you if necessary,' he said.

'What do you want me to do?' I asked.

The Minister hesitated.

'Well, I hardly know, except that I should like you to see the fellow and beat his price down. Maybe you could scare him?*

I shook my head.

'That kind of man isn't easily scared,' said I. 'He is evidently a thoroughly bad lot, and, being a policeman or an ex-policeman, as he will be in a day or two, he knows the law just as well as I, and he would be a difficult man to bluff. Now, if you'll be advised by me, Mr. Tresham, you will not say a word to Lord Colesun as to having seen or employed me.'

'But what can you do?' he asked. 'You do not even know the policeman's address.'

'I'll make a few inquiries which will help me to clear up the mystery of the drunken people.'

'Mystery?' he said. 'There was no mystery about it; they were there.'

'Exactly,' said I with a smile: 'but that is the mystery. Don't you realise, Mr.

Tresham, that in gaming houses drunkenness is as rare as at a revival meeting?'

I thereupon left him and pursued my investigation.

Scotland Yard very kindly gave me a few particulars, and the Home Office the necessary permission to see the proprietor of the raided gambling-house. He was in Wandsworth Gaol, and to Wandsworth I drove, handed in my order, and was taken to where a stout, elderly man sat on the edge of his seat.

'I want to talk to you about this raid of yours,' said I. 'How did they come to catch you?'

'How? Why, I was given away,' he said vehemently, 'and what's more, I know the man that gave me away.'

'Who was it?' I asked.

'You find out,' he snapped. 'I name no names; I keep my opinions to myself. I was running one of the quietest, best-conducted little joints in London, and it's a shame they couldn't leave me alone.'

'I like your idea of well-conducted little joints,' said I, and in a few brief words I gave him my own opinion of the class of establishment he kept.

'That's a lie,' he said. 'If there were a lot of lushers lying about don't you think the police would have brought it out?

'Anyway, I'm glad they raided me when they did, if they were going to raid at all,' he went on. 'If they'd come a couple of hours later we should have been in full swing. As it was, they caught a few. The police messed it, as they mess everything. Fancy raiding a gaming house at half-past nine at night!' he said contemptuously. 'You're a split, aren't you?'

'I am a sort of detective,' I admitted.

'Well, don't think I've got anything against the police, because I haven't,' he said. 'Inspector Ericson was decent to me, and I don't suppose he'd have raided me, if that swine hadn't given me away. I'll "Bart" him when I come out.'

'What name was that?' I said quickly.

'Never mind,' he replied evasively, and try as I did, he could not be induced to say any more.

Now, Inspector Ericson is one of the straightest men in London. No Robespierre was more incorruptible. He was certainly not the kind of man who would accept a thousand pounds to allow a detected gambler to go scot free.

Ericson was not at the station when I called, and I took the liberty of driving over to his house, and found him preparing to go on night duty.

'I wanted to see you, inspector, about the raid you made the other night.'

'Oh, did you?' he said, with his hard little smile.

'When you made the raid why did you choose half-past nine?'

'Well, the raid was made in accordance with instructions we received from headquarters. The gentleman who gave the house away told us that at half-past nine it was crowded, and, what's more, he had arranged with the doorkeeper to let us in at that hour.'

'Another question, Ericson. When you made the raid, did anybody offer you a thousand pounds to let them out?'

'I think not. Otherwise it would have been as good as paying me to put them in!' he said.

'I happen to know,' said I, 'that the gentleman who gave you the information which led to the raid was Lord Colesun.'

'You do, do you?' said he. 'Ah, well, you know a lot!'

'Well, I won't ask you whether it was he or somebody else,' said I. 'But tell me this—was your informant present when the raid was made?'

'I can answer you very emphatically that he was not,' replied Ericson.

'Just one more question, Inspector. Do you know whether there are any other gambling houses in Montacute Square?'

'I can tell you that there are not,' said the inspector, 'it is funny you should ask that. It was the same question asked by one of my detective-sergeants who was watching the place we raided. He reported that a lot of people had gone in to No. 27. The house we raided was No.43, farther along. He went over to make an inquiry, but found there was a fancy-dress ball on or something. In fact, he mistook a dressed-up policeman, as he thought, who was going into the house as a real one.'

The Vampire of Wembley

'Thank you, that's all I want to know,' said I, and went back to the office to get the report of my assistants, who had spent that afternoon making inquiries in knowledgeable circles in the city.

Their reports were very satisfactory from my point of view, and I was in the midst of reading them when Mr. Tresham rang through and asked me to come and see him.

'I hope I haven't annoyed you, Mr. Dixon, but I have had to tell Lord Colesun. I thought it was hardly fair to him. Will you come over?'

'Is he with you?' I asked.

'He is with me now.'

I gathered up the reports and read the last two on my way to Whitehall. Lord Colesun I had not met before.

He shook hands with me warmly on my introduction.

'Glad to meet you, Mr. Dixon. I have heard about you, and I am extremely glad that my friend Mr. Tresham has called you in. I was a little ratty when I heard in the first place, but since then I agree that it was wise to take professional advice. Mr. Tresham and I have been talking the matter over, and we have decided that the best thing to do is to pay this infernal policeman and let the matter rest.'

'I think it is the best thing to do,' broke in Mr. Tresham. 'I did have a wild idea that it would be better if you met the policeman, but on consideration I have decided that Bart—Lord Colesun—should carry the thing through himself.'

'I never expected to meet this policeman,' said I. 'At least, not in his role as a policeman. You said, Mr. Tresham, that although you did not see the policeman's face you noticed that he had one of his front teeth broken.'

Mr. Tresham nodded. I turned to Lord Colesun.

'May I ask you,' I said, 'if you know any person who has a front tooth broken?'

'I probably know several. I don't notice the teeth of policemen, however.'

'I am not talking about policemen,' I insisted. 'Do you know any other person with a broken front tooth?'

I had seen the young man's face change, and now he picked up his hat from a settee and walked towards the door.

'I'd like you to excuse me for a little while; I'm not feeling very well,' he said in a low voice.

'Wait!' said I, 'I have to finish my story.'

'Then you'll finish it alone,' snarled the man at the door, and went out, slamming it behind him.

The Minister looked at me in bewilderment.

'What does it all mean.'

'It means this,' said I. 'Your friend Lord Colesun has for months been on the verge of bankruptcy. Moreover, he has been taking funds from a company with which he is connected, which must be made good by tomorrow morning.'

'Good God! You don't suggest—' he began.

'I suggest that the gambling hell and the supposed police raid were got up for your special benefit. The gamblers and the police were members of a provincial touring company, who were brought to London to play their part by Lord Colesun, who told them that he was having a joke on one of his friends. The house was hired furnished—'

'But why the drunkenness?' asked Mr. Tresham.

'That was intended to make you all the more disgusted and all the more anxious to keep your name out of the case. To make the deception seem more real, your friend arranged for a gaming club, which undoubtedly existed in Montacute Square, to be raided the same night—as a matter of fact, an hour and a half before the sham raid was made. The policeman with the broken tooth was Lord Colesun's valet.'

'Then you suggest,' said Mr. Tresham in a low voice, 'that Bart was blackmailing me, and that the fifty thousand pounds was for himself?'

'I not only suggest that, but I advance it as a fact,' said I. 'The valet is a man who has been hand-in-glove with his Lordship in every dirty piece of business in which he has been engaged. Your friend arranged for a raid on a genuine gaming club in order that you should be able to read something in the next day's paper. The sham police who "raided" were in one of the rooms downstairs waiting until you were safely inside the saloon.'

The Minister sat at his desk, his head on his hands. At last he rose.

'Well, Mr. Dixon,' he said with a smile, 'you have saved me fifty thousand pounds, but you have cost me a very dear illusion.'

'You will not prosecute, of course?' said I.

He shook his head.

'If there is any of his father's spirit in the man, there will be no necessity for a prosecution,' he said quietly.

Tresham was right as it happened, for the first announcement I read when I opened my paper the following morning was that Lord Colesun had shot himself.

The Devil Light

I

Some men have an aversion to cats, others shrink back in horror from a third floor window and fight desperately to overcome the temptation to throw themselves into the street below. For others the mirror holds a devil who leers a man on to self-destruction. But for Hans Richter that cruel and puzzling light which he interpreted into E Flat held all that there was of threat and fear.

If you say that the obsession of little Hans savoured of madness, tell me something of yourself. Squeak a knife-edge along a plate, or knife-edge against knife-edge and watch the people shudder and grimace. They also are mad of the same madness. Some men and women grow frantic at the rustle of silk; others may not pass their palms over certain surfaces (such as plush or velvet) without a shivering fit. Exactly why, nobody knows.

There are undreamt of horrors in commonplace objects for some of us—Hans Richter had the advantage of hating and fearing that which was not commonplace.

He played second violin at the Hippoleum. He had little spare time with a daily matinée and a twelve o'clock rehearsal every Monday, but he utilized that spare time with great profit, being a most earnest student of colour values, and, moreover, a worshipper of heroes.

You had no doubt as to what manner of heroes qualified for his adoration. Nature had built him short and clumsy, with a pink, round face and blue eyes. She had built him cheap as a builder runs up a cottage out of the material left over from a more pretentious job.

'Well buttressed, but poorly thatched,' he described himself, and indeed the great Dame had been mean in the matter of head-covering, for his hair, sandy and fine, was in a quantity less than was necessary. His moustaches were mere wisps, but in the shape to which he trained them you read his mind, his faith and his pride.

He was a gentle soul, with strange and unusual views on lights, and a certain pride in his intimate knowledge of London. It was his boast that there was not a street in the metropolitan area which he had not visited, not a historic monument upon which he could not enlarge at length; and once on a more than ordinarily poisonous night of fog he had led Sam Burns by the hand from Holborn Town-Hall to Paddington Station, and never bungled a single crossing, never so much as mistook the entrance of a blind alley, though the fog was so thick that Sam could neither see his guide nor the pavement under his feet.

Oh, no, he was no spy—he hated the Prussian, as so many Bavarians did before the war (he was from Nurnberg). He was German all through, but neither favoured bureaucracy nor militarism.

They lived together, this curious pair, in a tiny house off Church Street, Paddington—in a neighbourhood of strange smells and of Sunday morning markets. Sam Burns was 'Mr Burns' in law, and entitled (did they but know it) to the respectful salute of policemen, for he was a naval gunner on the reserve of officers, and held the King's warrant.

They had one quality in common—that they were simple men — and because of this No 43 Bebchurch Street was a haven of peace.

For Sam directed such casual help as he could secure in his best quarter-deck manner, had a gift for spying out untidy corners and hurried scrubbings, a vigilance which earned for him the hatred and slander of the charladies of Paddington, and resulted in a constant melancholy procession of new servants.

They sat together by an open window on a Sunday evening in June 1914, taking the air. Sam's lean red face was one great scowl, for he was reading a thrilling murder case—facial contortion was part of the process of his reading.

'Murder's a curious thing,' he said at last, setting the paper down on his knee. 'I've killed men in my time—natives and that sort of thing—but always in what I might term the heat of battle. I wonder how it feels?'

Hans turned his mild face to the other and stared through his gold-rimmed glasses.

'Herr Gott!' he said. 'That you should talk about such subjects, Sam—who could think of murder on such a night? It is a night for thought—exalted thought!'

He stopped suddenly, pursing his lips and looking thoughtfully out of the open window, and upward to the patch of western sky which showed above the mean housetops.

'G minor,' he said abstractedly, and Sam grinned.

'You're mad on lights, Hans!" he chuckled. 'G minor!—what the dickens is G minor?'

Without turning his head or relinquishing his gaze the musician whistled a soft sweet note sustained, and full of sorrow.

Sam frowned.

'I'm beginning to see,' he admitted, 'yes—that's the kind of light it is. You're a crank on lights, Hans—'

The other swung round in his chair and reached for his violin and bow that lay on the table near him. He drew the bow across the muted strings and a gloomy stream of thick sound filled the little room.

'Purple,' he said, and played another long note—a joyous blatant note of arrogant triumph.

'Scarlet,' he smiled, and put the instrument back.

'Lights are horrible or beautiful—terrifying or adorable – listen.'

He seized the instrument again and sent the bow rasping across the strings.

'For God's sake don't make that infernal noise!' growled Sam shifting uneasily, for the note shrill and menacing carried terror in its volume.

Hans had the instrument on his knees. His lids were narrowed, his plump jaw outthrust.

'That is white light—the devil's light—cruel and searching. It stares and shrieks at me. There is a beckoning devil in that light. You see it on the stage—I have seen it a hundred times. It strips young girls of their modesty, it reveals the lie, it mocks the passé. You can see them staring at it—blinded and yet staring, their white teeth glittering, their red lips smiling like children smile when they are in pain—it is the light of war, and cruelty and suffering—phew!'

He flung the violin away and mopped his damp forehead with a big green handkerchief.

Sam rose from his window chair slowly.

'Hans, you're a fool,' he said, 'and I'm going to put a B major match to the A flat lamp.'

Hans laughed and rose too with the remark:

'And I'm going to a ten o'clock rehearsal—the show opens to-morrow—Gott! It is a quarter to ten already!'

*

It was not a happy rehearsal for the little German. There was a new American producer at the Hippoleum, a burly man in a grey sweater, who was quick to wrath, and had a wealth of unpleasant language.

In the third scene the lights went wrong. Four specially erected electric projectors had been fixed in the gallery, and on a certain chord, at the end of a song number, they had to concentrate upon the principal, who was singing. And they just didn't. One wandered off to the second entrance. One wavered undecidedly too far up stage, and the other two did not appear at all.

'Say, what's the matter with you?' exploded the producer. 'Are you crazy up there? Is this a joke?'

He said other sarcastic things, and said them through a megaphone, which somehow made them worse.

A hollow and apologetic voice answered from the deserted gallery.

'Put all your lines down—now put 'em on the proscenium arch—now put 'em all together up stage—now put 'em on the bald-headed fiddler in the orchestra—'

There was a gentle titter of laughter from the weary chorus—but it was short-lived.

The bald-headed fiddler was standing up facing the light, his face distorted with rage, his wild eyes glaring like a trapped animal, as his clawing hands flung out at the light.

A torrent of words, German and English, poured from his twisted mouth.

'Take it off! Take it off! Take it off!' he screamed.

There was an instant and a painful pause. The lights dimmed and an outraged producer strode down the central aisle of the theatre and confronted the second violin.

'For the lord's sake!' he said, mildly enough, 'have you gone mad, mister?'

The little man, one trembling hand curved about the orchestra rail, shook his head. He was very white, and the American, a judge of men, and kindly enough out of business hours, dropped his big hand on the other's shoulder.

'You go right along home and have a sleep, son,' he said gently; 'don't you worry—go right along home.'

'It's the light, sir,' faltered Hans, and blinked fearfully up at the gallery. I do not like the light—'

'Sure!' soothed the other; 'now you go right away and have a rest — there's nothin' comin' to you, son—on the square. I get just crazy like that myself.'

Hans did not lose his job—he played second fiddle on the opening night of that brilliant success, There You Are, Bunny! and would have gone on playing through the inevitable run but for certain great happenings in Europe. A prince of an Imperial house was killed, and when the message came to six chancelleries six separate and distinct ministers demanded of their war offices, 'How soon can you mobilize?'

Hans did not know this, but later he was to have misgivings.

'I must go home,' he said doggedly. 'I am too old to be of any use — but who knows?'

He looked wistfully at the red-faced Mr Burns, who sprawled across the table gloating over a newspaper chart which showed the relative proportions of the world's fleets.

Sam looked up.

'They'll want me,' he said with quiet satisfaction. 'My old captain will hoist his flag—he's vice admiral now—and he promised me that if ever there was a kick-up he'd take me. Who made the Penelope the best gunnery ship in the home fleet? Me, Hans!'

He thumped his thick chest and his eyes were puckered with proud laughter.

'I'm not too old for sea-going, but if I am there are lots of jobs for a man who ain't too old to spot a damned—'

He stopped in confusion. The eyes of Hans were set and the dominant expression in those eyes was envy.

'Gott!' he said with a sigh, 'I am no good—I hate war — it is terrible to think about—it is like the white light, a devil! But I must go back. Perhaps I may take the place of one—if He wants me!'

He left the next day—an exhilarating day for Mr Burns, for he had received a notification that 'my lords of the Admiralty' had accepted his offer of service.

Hans, with his brown ulster and his aged violin, came, packed his cheap gripsack and two brown paper parcels, paid his share of the expenses which were current, and went off in a taxicab.

'Good-by, Sam.'

'Good-by, Hans—good luck!'

The little man's grief was undisguised.

'I shall think of you—as a soft golden light, Sam,' he choked.

'That's right,' replied his less imaginative friend, 'yellow for me, Hans.'

Poor old Hans! So thought Mr Gunner Burns with a sigh...anyway, they weren't likely to meet. The little musician would scarcely be found amongst the ships' companies which the marksmanship of Gunner Burns foredoomed to destruction.

So passed Hans, and as for Sam, after a spell at Whale Island teaching the young and impetuous naval marksman how to shoot, he came back to Somewhere in England to more important duties.

II

There was a noise like the roll of a trap drum—an even 'br-r-r-r' of sound.

Gunner Burns standing in the darkness, dropped his head sideways and listened.

It was faint at first, but grew louder with every second that passed, and the noise came from the air.

Sam peered over the parapet in a swift, keen scrutiny of the sector south of the position. Somewhere beyond the inky belt of darkness which blotted out the nearest features of the landscape was London—London the vast and wealthy, a gigantic, flat hive buzzing and droning, unconscious of the danger.

As the watcher looked he pressed the electric button which was fixed to the wall near his hand, and almost instantly a second figure joined him.

The trap drum noise was now loud and angry, and the men craned their necks and searched the skies through their night glasses.

'There she is, sir!' said Sam in a low voice, 'the biggest they've got ... '

The officer at his side had his glasses on the lean shape that blotted no more than two or three stars at a time.

'What's her range?' he asked with the regret in his voice of one who anticipates an answer which will dash his hopes.

'Three or four thousand yards—shall I light her up?'

The other's hands had closed on the telephone receiver in the little recess beneath the parapet.

' 'Lo—that you, Shepherds Bush? Zep coming over, I'm going to light her up—no, only one as far as I can see. She'll start circling in a minute, looking for the small-arms factory as usual...Right!'

He turned to the man at his side with a grunted order. Something hissed and spluttered. Little bubbles of light outlined a big barrel shape somewhere in the rear of where he stood, and there leaped into the air a solid white beam of dazzling light which moved restlessly from side to side till it settled on something which looked for all the world like a silver cigar.

'She's just beyond range—but give her one for herself, Burns,' said the young officer. 'She's turning!'

The deafening crash of a gun woke the still night—a drift of smoke passed between the observer and his objective. As it cleared a tiny point of vivid light flicked and faded beneath the big silver cigar.

'Five hundred yards short,' was the bitter comment.

'She'll take some hitting! Keep the light on her—Shepherds Bush will pick her up in a minute...'

WHOOM!

The shock and pulsation of the explosion came to them. The trees rustled as though they had been stirred by a gust of wind, and the concrete parapet under the officer's hands trembled and shook again.

The old gunner at his side drew a sharp breath.

'Addlestone—that is!' he said. 'Fancy Addlestone! Good God, it doesn't seem real, does it? Why, when I was a kid I went to school at Addlestone...'

Another report followed, fainter than the first, and then over toward Addlestone came a red glow in the sky, a glow which gathered in brightness until it was almost golden.

'Them thermite bombs are pretty useful,' said the gunner with reluctant admiration. 'Hot! You can't get near a fire that's been started by one of them. I've seen men and women roasted to death by 'em, and they never knew what killed 'em. There's Shepherds Bush, sir!'

From the south two white beams had shot into the air and focused instantly on the fast moving cigar. She turned to the westward, and the lights followed. She moved in one majestic sweep to the east—but the lights did not leave her. They were the two great eyes of the dark world staring their wrath at the night bird.

'She wants that cloud dam' badly,' said the young naval officer. 'Put your light over the cloud—yes, it's big enough.'

He took up the telephone.

' 'Lo, Shepherds Bush...She's going for the cloud on the left. She's about level—no, I can't keep her lit up for much longer—she's getting beyond my range.'

The sky shape was now blurred and indistinct, for it had reached the misty edges of the cloud—in ten seconds it had disappeared. But now flashed into the air not two but a dozen searching eyes. They grew from the dark void beyond the hillcrest to the south, slender white spokes of light that criss-crossed incessantly. The cloud glowed yellow where the beam came to a dead end, and once it sparkled at a dozen points, For all the world, as Gunner Burns said, as if some one were striking a match along its under surface and had done no more than raise a shower of sparks.

'Shrapnel,' said the old authority approvingly; 'that'll rattle her a bit. Nothing like a nearby shell burst to make you take your eyes from the compass—there she is!'

Out she came from the same cloud-wall into which she had dived — into the gleam and glare of the searchlights. Left and right, beneath and at the side of her the light splashes came and went. They were as soft and as sudden as the glow the fireflies make.

The great machine turned again, her nose rose slowly into the air and her tail went down. The watchers could see the cloud of oily smoke at the stern as her speed increased.

'She's got to climb for it, and climb quick,' said the gunner.

A quick fan of light leapt up from the ground over by Golders Green. WHOOM!

'A keepsake,' said the lieutenant grimly.

The telephone bell tinkled and an urgent voice demanded his immediate attention.

'She's going back to you, Carter—keep your light on her. She's twelve thousand seven hundred feet up and rising—shoot her off or she'll give you hell!'

'Ay, ay, sir!' the officer swung round. 'Light her up!'

Again the searchlight stabbed the dark, and again the cigar floated in a halo of soft radiance.

Then from the north came a new sound. It was not the 'br-r-r' they had heard before, but a purring note—a far-off motorcycle could reproduce the gentle din.

High above, the merest midgets in the vast space of starlit sky, three specks of earth-dust moved slowly across the field of the watchers' vision, and as they moved, in the limitless dome of the heavens a red ball of light lived and died. The young officer sought the telephone.

'Three aeroplanes up—they have signalled "shut down searchlights,"' he called breathlessly.

Two seconds passed, and then, as though one hand controlled the light shafts that swept the skies, they vanished.

They waited in the dark. The never-ceasing roar of the Zeppelin engines neither increased nor grew fainter. She was cruising laterally for some reason—the Golders Green telephone explained.

'We've hit her, sir—first or second compartment. Think one of her fore tractor screws is out of action...Yes, she got near us, but now she's drifting your way.'

'Her fourth visit,' said Sam.

'And every time she's gone straight to the place she wanted to reach,' added the officer with an impatient and wondering little 'ch'k' of his tongue. 'That fellow must know London like a book—he must know it blind to pick out his target with all the lights shaded and faked.'

Sam nodded and thought of a certain Hans Richter.

Poor old Hans! Fancy making Hans the focus of ten three-thousand candle-power searchlights! Sam grinned in the darkness.

Three...four...five minutes passed, then from the sky shot a thin beam of light that seemed from the viewpoint of the gun position to be aimed horizontally from the airship.

'Got her blinders on,' commented Sam. 'Aeroplanes are up to her level—there they are! Right ahead of her! They can do nothing with the light in their faces. She'll climb if she ain't climbing already.'

Another minute passed. Then a speck of red fire appeared in the black heavens, another red followed and then a green.

'Aeroplanes coming down—she's blinded 'em,' he said rapidly. 'Stand by to light her up—keep 'em off the aeroplanes...Now!'

From every point of the horizon the beams sprang until the sky was a thick jungle of converging light stalks. They beat fiercely, remorselessly, upon the big cigar as she zigzagged her way to safety and the north-west.

A thousand feet above the guns the landing lights of an aeroplane burnt blue, and the great bird swooped to earth. They ran out to him as the guns of Golders Green began a frantic bombardment of the disappearing Zeppelin.

It was Burns who helped the pilot to alight, and the boy who jumped to the ground was shaking from head to foot.

'Did you see it...did you see it?' he croaked. 'It was awful!'

They got him to the shelter of the position and to the little room behind. The airman was pinched and blue of face, but it was not his cold ride which had set him a tremble. He drank the cup of hot coffee they gave him, and as he did so his teeth were chattering against the edge of the mug.

'Awful!' he said at last; 'did you see it?'

'The Zep?'

He shook his head impatiently.

'No—after we gave the signal for the light, and they all came up—we were under the angle, and I looked up and suddenly a man—' he shivered and closed his eyes, 'a man leaped and straight out of the fore cabin...leaped and turned over and over...'

*

In the morning they made a search and found, in the big Mill Pond by Addlestone one who had in his lifetime been Hans Richter — the man who knew London and hated lights. Especially lights that could be translated into E flat.

Edgar Wallace

The Man from the Stars

IN THE SUMMER of 1915, I received a request from Berlin which somewhat surprised me. I was instructed to send to Holland as many good maps of London as I could buy, and I was told also to prepare one special map, marking the areas which the street-lamps had been darkened. This was followed (or it may have come I the same dispatch, I forget) by a request that I should instruct my men to discover how it was that the British Government knew we contemplated an air-raid on London.

I myself wondered what information the British Government had secured and how they had secured it. For months the streets had been lit as gaily as pre-war days. The theatre signs glowed and flashed, the West End streets were bathed in radiance and then, almost by a touch of the magician's wand London "went dark." Street lamps were shaded, the light signs outside the theatres were extinguished and it was almost impossible to pick your way through the streets.

I suppose my excellent friend, the High-Born Baron von Hertz-Missenger would have said, "English Secret Service." He reminds me of a character Charles Dickens the great English poet, who invariably thought that his head was the head of King Charles II!

The explanation I offered was, that some of our too impetuous airmen must have betrayed the fact by shouting with haughty insolence to the English airmen they met in the air. As this has never been denied, it is probably true.

At any rate I set myself to work upon a map. It was a long business, and very unsatisfactory, because the whole of London was dark, and no place was more light the another. This I reported, forwarding the maps by special courier.

And then I received a request from our Headquarters that I should arrange light-signals which should be seen by Zeppelins. The idea was to post three lights so that they formed a triangle, one near Albany Park, one near Maidstone Road, and a third in the east, near Shepherd's Junction. The triangle thus made would contain all the valuable city area which it was our

The Vampire of Wembley

Zeppelins' intention to utterly destroy.

Of the first raid in September, it is not necessary for me to tell. Of how the cowardly Englishmen trembled beneath the midnight hail of bombs, you have read. I myself did not witness the raid, because, on receiving information on the afternoon Zeppelins were due, I had left London for Cornwall. Since it was impossible for the brave fellows who piloted our good Zeppelins to distinguish between a patriot and a hateful enemy, I thought that in the interest of the Fatherland, it was necessary that I should be as far away as possible when the dread visitation came.

I returned to London the next morning and arrived at eleven o'clock. Oh what consternation there was. Oh what vile language these unkultured Londoners used, what epithets, what adjectives, the A's, and B's, and C's, and D's, they called us—but of that anon!

I was in some anxiety before my journey's end was reached as to whether I should have to walk a part of the journey, and I was greatly relieved on questioning the conductor to learn that Paddington Station had escaped the holocaust. When I arrived at Paddington everything was going on as usual. To my amazement buses were running and cabs were plying for hire.

"Where was the raid ? " I asked.

"In the East End and the City," was the reply. So, I thought, my triangle had proved efficacious, and calling a cab, I said: "Will you please drive me to the ruined area?"

The poor, ignorant fellow thought at first that it was the name of a public-house, and I bad to enlighten him.

"Where the bombs struck," I said.

"Oh, yes," he said, brightening up, "I will ask a policeman where they fell."

"Do you mean to tell me," I inquired, "that you don't know? Perhaps you haven't been to the City?"

"Yes sir," he replied in the true boorish cabman spirit. "I've been to the city three times but I ain't seen no place where the bombs fell."

This of course was "eye-wash." For my part I had removed all my archives from my office, and as that was on the edge of the City, I drove there first and as pleased to find that my office had not been touched. I drove up Ludgate Hill and apparently everything was as usual, and it was not until he had driven farther on and. had penetrated a side street that I saw the wreckage of a house. It was pleasing and yet disappointing. A number of windows had been smashed, one house was in ruins and there was a big hole in a court-yard, but the damage was as such as might have been caused by an explosion of gas.

It took me a long time before I found the second place where a bomb had fallen, and there again the results were not as I expected. I spent the whole of that day wandering about looking for devastation. I went east and south, and north, and although I saw some damaged houses, the results of our gallant Zeppelins' visit left much to be desired.

Returning to my office I was called on the phone and a code message was sent through to me. As I expected, it was from Berlin asking for full particulars of the damage done, and very faithfully I described what I had seen, coded it and passed it on to the proper quarters.

To my wrath and humiliation, the next evening brought a peremptory demand from Berlin. It had been sent by radio, picked up off the coast by a little steamer plying the flag of —, and was brought to me from an East Coast port by one of he couriers we employed for that purpose. The message was, as I say, peremptory, and there were tears in my eyes, tears of sorrow and injury as I read it.

"Cannot understand your message. Our pilots report Westminster Abbey as bombed. Whole streets of the City are in flames, Houses of Parliament partly destroyed, also London Bridge and Tower of London. Several ships in docks hit and sunk. Please personally investigate and report."

Of course there was a chance that these cunning English had, by means of scene painters and workmen labouring through the night, removed all sign of the destruction, but I walked over London Bridge without any difficulty, and as far as I could see the Tower of London was uninjured.

I reported the same, and three days later, had this message back:

"Be on south side of Three Mile Wood, north-north-east Saffron Walden, at eleven o'clock on the night of October 7th."

I could not understand this message, and my new assistant, who had arrived from America, Herr Wilhelm Peters, was as much puzzled as I. However, on the 7th of October, I journeyed to Saffron Walden, which is a little town in Essex, and by studying a map I discovered that Three Mile Wood was inaccurately named because it was about seven miles from the town. I decided to walk, and arrived in the neighbourhood of the wood at about ten o'clock at night. Having ascertained by consulting my compass which was the south side, I made my way across fields and muddy ditches to a big meadow which was exactly placed to the south of the sparsely-wooded little forest.

It was a clear night with a thin ground haze and was rather cold. I had brought one of those walking-sticks, the top of which forms a seat, and this found very comfortable; for the inner man I had a flask of brandy and some liver sandwiches, and I settled myself down to my vigil, wondering what on earth ad induced Headquarters to send me upon this wild adventure.

Then suddenly my heart began beating at a tremendous rate as I divined the reason ! It was intended this night for our airships to reach London, and they desired that I should be a witness. What folly! What folly! What incomparable insanity to risk the life of a high Officer of Intelligence, to place him in such horrible jeopardy. I felt myself grow pale, but then with an effort I braced up. I was a German!

We Germans fear God and nothing else, and, besides, I thought there might not be an air-raid after all.

But what satisfaction I got out of that thought was quickly dissipated. Suddenly an ominous sound came to me. A double "boom! " far away an the east, was followed by three staccato explosions. Another bomb fell, suddenly the whole of the eastern sky was illuminated by the tracing fingers of searchlights.

"Boom!" The sound was growing nearer and my mouth was dry. I was choking. I loosened my collar and mopped the sweat from my forehead and stood up, my knees trembling.

Edgar Wallace

I have thought the matter over since and I have come to the conclusion that my agitation might be explained in this way, that I was trembling with pride in the fearless exploits of our gallant airmen, those intrepid messengers of death who sailed the midnight skies fearless of foe; that I perspired because the liver sandwich was perhaps a little too highly flavoured. Anyway, the cursed things were corning closer and who knows what mistakes a blundering fool of a pilot might make. The searchlights were suddenly extinguished, the guns were silent and for ten minutes I heard no sound save a faint but ever-growing-nearer hum of an engine in the sky. Then there was a shrieking whistle, a crash that seemed to shake the very earth, a blinding fan of flame and, then silence.

In my rage I shook my fist at the sky.

"Stupid jackasses, miserable, bat-eyed swine-hound! " I cried. "Have you not the highest instructions in your pockets to avoid bombing an Intelligence Officer?"

The cursed thing passed overhead. It was roaring like a railway train passing through a tunnel. I saw the bulk of it outlined against the stars and then I saw something else, a little black dot that moved and swayed against the sky. I thought it might be some infernal machine and I nearly fainted.

Understand that my chief thought was of Germany. I had no fear for myself, I was merely a cog in the wheel of the great machine and stood ready at any hour and all days to sacrifice myself for our dear Deutschland. Fortunately, there was a fallen tree in my neighbourhood, and under this I crept, looking out from time to time to see what had happened to the strange thing in the air.

Then I heard a thud, a rustle, and an oath, and I jumped up, bruising the back of my head against the tree-trunk, and ran towards the sound, for that oath was in good German.

"Wer da?" called a sharp voice. "It is I, Heine," I replied.

"Oh, good," said the voice in German. "You are on the spot, I see. Help free me from this doubly rotten parachute."

I made my way to him and helped unbuckle some of the straps that fastened him, and presently he was free.

"Have you got a pocket lamp?" he asked. "No, perhaps you had better not use it. Where can I put the parachute?"

I suggested the tree under which I had been—I won't say hiding, let me rather say taking cover.

"Have you a car?" he asked.

"No," I replied.

"You are an ass," said he; "why haven't you a car?"

I knew by the imperiousness of his tone that he was a true German gentleman probably highly born and connected by many social ties with an old family of Prussia.

"I am the Baron von Treutzer," he said, as though answering my thoughts "and I have been sent here to survey the damage that was done in the last raid."

"Your Excellency will discover that I have spoken nothing but the truth," I said humbly. The sound of the Zeppelin's engines, which had diminished, was now increasing in volume.

"Is the airship returning?" I asked.

"Yes, yes," he said testily. He took from his pocket a small electric lamp and flashed it three times in the air and immediately after three tiny sparks of light showed in the sky.

"They won't be dropping any more bombs, Herr Baron?" I asked carelessly.

"Good heavens! What does it matter if they do? " he boomed—he was a booming kind of man, born to command, typical of our virile aristocracy which has placed Germany in the forefront of world-nations.

"I only asked," I said. "I am a mere observer."

"We only dropped a few bombs," he said, "just to explain our presence. The real business of our visit is here." I heard him slap his chest in the darkness.

"I did not know where the raid was intended," I said, "or I would have arranged for a leader."

"A leader?" he asked. "What the devil do you mean?"

"Evidently Herr Baron is not a member of the Zeppelin crew," I said humbly, "or he would know that the Zeppelins are 'led' to their destination by motor-cars with strong head-lamps."

"Of course I am not a member of the Zeppelin crew," he said in deep disgust, "I am a Royal Lieutenant of the 31st Regiment of the Prussian Guard."

"Does your Excellency intend staying here very long?" I asked, as we trudged along the country road.

"For a week," he replied, "after that I return —"

"By—?"

"That is my business," he replied, "if a Zeppelin can bring me here, a Zeppelin can take me away."

Though I had never heard of parachutes that go up, I know all things are possible owing to the inventive genius of our nation, so I questioned him no further. Outside Saffron Walden we stopped while I went to the hotel to collect the handbag which I had left there.

Needless to say the people in the hotel were in that condition of cowardly funk which our Zeppelin always inspires. The children were crying because they had not seen the airship, and again I heard in the common bar of the hotel those terrible words which my modesty would only allow me to designate by using certain letters of the alphabet.

I rejoined the Baron and we made our way to the railway station, which was in darkness. Fortunately the train which came in was also darkened and remained that way until we reached London and I was able to bring the Baron to my flat without observation. He was a tall, handsome gentleman, dressed in civilian clothes of a noble cut and rich texture, and over a glass of whisky he graciously unbent and told me that he had come to England by this curious method to discover the extent of the damage, not only of the first raid, but of a raid which was projected and by which it was hoped to lay London entirely in ruins.

"On what day will that occur? " I asked.

"You will be notified in due time. It may be to-morrow, and it may be the next day," he replied.

"I only asked," I said carelessly, "because it is necessary for me to see one of my agents in North Devon one day this week, and I should not like to miss the raid."

"You will stay here until I go. That is an order. Why are you looking so pale?"

"It is the pressure of work, your Excellency," I replied. "I am afraid I have rather taxed my strength. My doctor suggested that I ought to go away at once to Cornwall or perhaps Scotland."

"We hope to bomb Scotland," said the Baron thoughtfully. "It would not be a bad idea if you were there."

"When I said Scotland," I said hastily, "I should have said that my doctor suggested I should go to Scotland in the spring. This of course is the very worst weather. Are you likely to bomb Wales?"

"We cannot reach there. It is beyond our reach," said the Baron.

"I only ask," I said, "because he also suggested that I should go there."

"When the raids are over you can go to the devil. I only want your assistance when they are on."

"Did you say raids or raid?" I asked.

"There may be two," he replied callously.

The next morning he expressed his intention of going through the City and the East End to photograph the worst of the damage. I did not offer to accompany him, and indeed, had he suggested that I should do so, I should have firmly declined. Fortunately, he knew London very well, for he had been an attaché the German Embassy a few years before the war broke out, so ha had no need my assistance or guidance.

He left the flat at eleven o'clock and I arranged to meet him at a restaurant in Piccadilly for lunch. I need hardly say that he was armed with a passport not only very completely filled in, but endorsed with an exact imitation of rubber stamps which were used in those days by examining officers at Folkestone when passengers landed.

I was waiting for him at one o'clock, but he did not arrive. Half-past one came, a quarter to two, two o'clock, and I began to feel seriously alarmed, and was thinking what an excellent text his arrest would provide for a letter to Potsdam on the futility of sending amateurs, when he came through the swing doors.

He uttered no word till we were sitting at the table, and the waiter had served the soup.

"These English people are very clever," he said at last.

"In a way they are clever," I said, "but by the side of the German—"

"Don't talk nonsense. Our German people are merely slavish imitators of everybody else in the world. If Germany was not a nation of slaves we should never have an army."

This put an end to the easy flow of conversation, but presently I ventured ask: "Why does your Excellency think the English are clever?"

"I am referring to the way they have cleared up the mess we made and have run up new buildings." He looked up at me curiously as he spoke.

"Don't you agree?"

"Naturally," I said heartily, "I have reason to believe that hundreds thousands of workmen have been working day and night to restore tube damage.'

He laughed.

"In addition to being a fool, you are a liar," he said, and I could only smile the good humour and buoyant frankness of this high-born officer who was in a probability in the entourage of the All-highest himself and, at any rate, as I have since learnt, had frequently dined with that exalted Prince whom we call the Hope of Germany.

"No," Baron von Treutzer went on, "the Zeppelin did little or no damage. It caused nothing of the smash that we expected it would. We will see what tonight's raid brings out."

"To-night?" I said, half-rising from my seat.

"Did I say to-night?" he said in an off-band way. "Well, whenever it happens."

But I knew that in a moment of incaution he had spoken the truth.

"By the way, I shall want you with me to-night," he said.

"To-night?" I repeated. "I am very sorry but this is the one night I can not be with your Excellency. I have an important messenger coming from Ireland with particulars of a rising, and the Foreign Office has particularly asked me—"

"I shall want you to-night," repeated the Herr Baron, "and you will meet me at ten o'clock, let us say, in St. Paul's Churchyard."

"Himmel! Herr Baron!" I exploded, "that would be in the very centre the raid!"

"Did I ever say that it would not?" he asked coolly, "Of course it will be in the centre of the raid. You understand, at ten o'clock. The War Office require a detailed account by eye-witnesses of the damage which is done,"

"But my messenger arrives at Fishguard to-night," I said with a tremor in my voice, "Forgive me if I am agitated, Herr Baron, but I realize the terrible importance, the absolute necessity, of meeting that boat."

"At ten o'clock you will be in St. Paul's Churchyard," said the Baron.

How I loathed and hated this tyrant. We Germans are naturally lovers of freedom. We despise the sycophant and the toady. Tyranny to us is a pestilential disease to be stamped out with an iron heel. Woe to those who endeavour to enslave the Germans, for they are biting on granite!

I told the Baron that I would meet him at the appointed time.

"Don't come before ten," he said. "We will remain until the raid is over."

I lifted my hat and bowed as I parted from him in Piccadilly, and I prayed most fervently, that the earth would open and swallow this pig, whose abominable manners and low attitude to men not so well born as himself (though of that I am not sure, for there were many stories about my mother's friendship for the Graf von Maldesee, which I sometimes reflect upon with a certain amount of satisfaction) aroused in me the deepest scorn.

I could eat no dinner that night, I could do no work that afternoon. I sat in my office until a quarter to ten, suffering, I think, from a touch of malaria and ague which I contracted in America. I arrived in St. Paul's Churchyard, dark and gloomy and silent, on the stroke of ten. I had arranged to meet the

Baron at the corner of one of the lanes which slope down to Upper Thames Street, and here I took my station.

At a quarter past ten he had not arrived. At twenty minutes past ten a hundred searchlights flashed into the sky and the first gun-shot woke the sleeping city. The Zeppelin was coming straight to the City, but was west of where I stood. I heard the thud of its bombs and the devil's chorus of the guns. I saw the skies speckled with shrapnel bursts, but much of what happened in that brief space of time between its appearance and its disappearance is blotted from my memory.

I could only stand crouched in a friendly doorway, my hands before my eyes, thinking of my dear friends, and particularly of a certain girl in Chicago with whom I had exchanged photographs, of my dear home, my little brothers, in fact all my life passed before me. I dare not go out to look for the Herr Baron.

How I envied him, that hardened man of war to whom this terrible concatenation of sound was as the gentle zephyrs; who could stand uncowed and watch with his stern military eye the destruction that was going on about him, uncaring, unafraid, contemptuous of danger, seeking only the information he required for his superiors!

In that moment I almost loved the man, even though I hated to meet him lest he mistook my ague for a more ignoble emotion, but presently I plucked up courage and went out to look for him. He was not at the corner of the lane nor was he on the pavement at all.

I made a circuit of the Cathedral without meeting him and then I realized that the Zeppelins had not been near St. Paul's but had passed westward. Naturally he would have been informed at the last moment and would have been on a spot where they would pass.

I did not attempt to join the throngs that gathered about the places where the bombs had fallen, but made my way homeward. At one o'clock he had not returned; two, three, and four passed. I still listened and then the horror of the possibility seized me. This gallant man had perhaps paid for his temerity with his life and I bought an early morning paper as soon as one was procurable and searched in vain for some indication of his fate.

Such a man could not be stricken down without attracting attention, but there was no reference whatever to such a one as he. In a fever of anxiety I paced my room. I called up my various agents but they could give me no information and I had almost abandoned hope when, at half-past eleven, the Baron came, debonair and calm, into my office.

"You had a good view," were the first words he said.

"Oh, Herr Baron," I said. I grasped his hand and shook it (a most presumptuous thing to do); "I am so glad to see you back! If you missed me I was on the spot."

"I didn't miss you," he said.

"Where were you?"

"I was at Fishguard, meeting your man, but apparently without success, for he did not come."

"You were at Fishguard?" I gasped.

"Naturally," he said, "you don't suppose I am such a silly fool that I am going to stand under a bomb to see it burst, do you?"

Such a man was this mean-souled dog, von Treutzer!

Thank heaven! He disappeared in a week. He may have been picked up by a descending Zeppelin. He may have been taken off by a near-approaching submarine. I have had no news, but if I hear he got back to Germany alive, I, Heine, will be sorry.

The Looker and the Leaper

FOLEY, the smoke-room oracle, has so often bored not only the members of the club, but a much wider circle of victims, by his views on heredity and the functions of the hormones—for he has a fluent pen and an entree to the columns of a certain newspaper that shall be—nameless—that one is averse to recalling his frayed theories.

He is the type of scientist who takes a correspondence course in such things as mnemonics, motor engineering, criminology, wireless telegraphy, and character-building. He paid nothing for the hormones, having found them in an English newspaper report of Professor Parrott's (is it the name?) lecture. Hormones are the little X's in your circulatory system which inflict upon an unsuspecting and innocent baby such calamities as his uncle's nose, his father's temper, and Cousin Minnie's unwholesome craving for Chopin and bobbed hair. The big fellows in the medical world hesitate to assign the exact function of the hormones or even to admit their existence.

Foley, on the contrary, is prepared to supply thumb-nail sketches and specifications. When you go to the writing-table in the "Silence" room, and find it littered with expensive stationery, more or less covered with scrawly-wags, it is safe betting that Foley has been introducing his new friend to some wretched member whom he has inveigled into an indiscreet interest.

But Hormones apart, there is one theory of evolution to which Foley has clung most tenaciously. And it is that the ultra- clever father has a fool for a son.

Whether it works the other way round he does not say. I should think not, for Foley senior is in his eightieth year, believes in spiritualism, and speculates on margins.

Foley advanced his theory in relation to Dick Magnus.

John Seymour Magnus, his father, is popularly supposed to be in heaven, because of the many good qualities and characteristics recorded on the memorial tablet in St. Mary's Church. Thus: He was a Good Father, a Loving Husband and a Faithful Friend, and performed Many Charitable Deeds in This City.

There is nothing on the memorial tablet about his Successful Promotions or Real Estate Acquisitions. He was bracketed first as the keenest business man of his day. A shrewd, cunning general of commerce, who worked out his plans to the minutest detail, he ran his schemes to a time-table and was seldom late. All other men (except one) would comprehend the beginning and fruition of their schemes within the space of months. John Seymour Magnus saw the culmination of his secret politics three years ahead.

There was one other, a rival, who had the same crafty qualities. Carl Martingale was his contemporary, and it is an important circumstance that he supplied, in his son, a complete refutation of all Foley's theories. Carl and John died within twelve days of one another, and both their great businesses went to only sons.

Dick took over the old man's chair, and was so oppressed by his uncongenial surroundings that he sold it for a ridiculous figure to Steven Martingale. The two were friends, so the sale was effected over a luncheon for which Dick paid.

Steven had arranged the lunch weeks ahead, had decided upon the course of conversation which would lead up to the question of sale, and had prepared his reply when Dick was manoeuvered into offering the property. For Steven was his parent, and worse. Old Carl was a selfmade boor, with no refined qualities. Steven had the appearance and speech of a gentleman and shared certain views on life with the anthropoid ape.

Ugly stories floated around, and once old Jennifer came into the club in a condition bordering on hysteria and drank himself maudlin. He had hoped to bag Steven for the family, and had allowed his pretty daughter Fay a very free hand.

Too free, it seems. Nothing happened which in any way discommoded Steven. The old fellow owed him an immense amount of money, and Steven knew to a penny the exact strength of these financial legirons.

He was a strikingly handsome fellow, the type the shop-girls rave about—dark, tall, broad of shoulder and lean of flank, an athlete and something of a wit. A greater contrast to Dick could not be imagined, for Dick was thinnish and small, fair haired, rather short-sighted (Steven's flashing eye and long lashes were features that fascinated) and languid.

But he did not develop his left-handedness until after he was married.

Both Dick and Steven courted Thelma Corbett, and never a day passed but that their cars were parked in the vicinity of the Corbett ménage. Corbett being on the danger-zone of bankruptcy was indifferent as to which of the two men succeeded in their quest, and Thelma was in a like case.

She was one of those pretty slender creatures whom. meeting, leave you with a vague unrest of mind. Where had you met her before? Then you realized (as I realized) that she was the ideal toward which all the line artists who ever drew pretty women were everlastingly striving. She was cold and sweet, independent and helpless, clever and vapid; you were never quite certain which was the real girl and which was the varnish and the finishing-school.

To everybody's surprise, she married Dick. Steven had willed it, of course. He half admitted as much one night between acts when we were smoking in the lobby of the Auditorium. Dick had at that time been married for the best part of a year and was childishly happy.

"I can't understand how Dick came to cut you out, Steven," I said. He was feeling pretty good toward me just about then, for I had pulled him through a sharp attack of grippe.

He laughed, that teasing little laugh of his.

"I thought it best," he said, a statement which could be taken two ways. That he was not exposing his modesty or displaying the least unselfishness, ho went on to explain:

"She was too young, too placid. Some women are like that. The men who marry them never wake them up. Some go through life with their hearts asleep and die in the belief that they have been happy. They have lived without 'struggle,' and only 'struggle' can light the fire which produces the perfect woman. I figured it that way."

I was silent.

"I figured it that way"—a favorite expression of his—explained in a phrase the inexplicable.

"That is why you find the most unlikely women running away with the most impossible men," he went on; "the heavens are filled with the woes of perfect husbands and the courts shudder with their lamentations. They are bewildered, stunned, outraged. They have showered their wealth and affection upon a delicate lady, and in return she has fled with a snubnosed chauffeur whose vocabulary is limited to twelve hundred words and whose worldly possessions are nil."

I said nothing, and soon after the bell rang and we went back to our seats.

The Vampire of Wembley

He drove me home that night and came up to my den for a drink, and I reopened the subject of Dick and his wife.

"Dick is one of Nature's waste products," he said. "He has neither initiative nor objective in life. How could old Magnus breed such a son? He was the cleverest, shrewdest, old devil in the City. Dick is just pap and putty—a good fellow and a useful fellow for holding my lady's wool or carrying my lady's Chow, but—"

He shook his head. "No 'struggle' there, Steve?" I asked. "Foley's theory works out in this case."

"Foley is a fool," smiled Steven. "What about me? Aren't I my father's son?" I admitted that.

"No, Dick lives from breakfast to supper, and could no more work out a scheme as his father did than I could knit a necktie."

"And there is no 'struggle' in the establishment?" I repeated, and he nodded gravely. "There is no 'struggle,'" he said, and although he never said the words I felt him saying "as yet."

Steven became a frequent visitor at the Magnus' house—Dick told me this himself. "He's an amusing person," he said—I met him in the Park, and he stopped his car to talk"—and I can't help feeling that life is a little dull for Thelma."

It was much duller for people who were brought much into contact with Thelma, but I did not say so. She was the kind of hostess who wanted entertaining.

Everybody loved Dick in those days, and he was welcomed wherever he went. Later, when he passed through that remarkably awkward stage, a stage which we usually associate with extreme adolescence, he was not so popular, and I was a little bit worried about him. It grieved me to see a man with all the money in the world making a playtime of life, because people who live for play can find their only recreation in work, and he never expressed the slightest desire to engage himself in the pursuit which had built up his father's colossal fortune. He rode well, he shot well, he played a good game of golf, and it was a case of "Let's get Dick" for a fourth at bridge.

"The fact is," said Dick, when I tackled him one day, "heavy thinking bores me. Maybe if I had to, I would. Sometimes I feel that I have a flash of my father's genius, but I usually work out that moment of inspiration in a game of solitaire.

"One afternoon he took me home to tea, arriving a little earlier than usual. He was evidently surprised to find Steve's car drawn up near the house. He should have been more surprised when he walked through the French windows opening from the lawn to the drawing-room, and found Steve and Thelma side by side on a settee examining Medici prints. It may have been necessary for the proper study of Art that Steve's hand should be upon the girl's shoulder. Evidently she did not think so, for she tried to disengage herself, but Steve, much more experienced in the ways of the world, kept his hand in position and looked up with a smile. As for me, I felt de trop.

"Hello, people!" said Dick, glaring benignly into the flushed face of the girl, "do my eyes behold a scandal in process of evolution? Or have I interrupted an exposition on the art of Michael Angelo?"

Steve rose with a laugh.

"I brought Thelma some pictures," he said, "they're a new lot just published; they are rather fine, don't you think?"

Dick looked at the pictures and, having no artistic soul, said that they struck him as a little old-fashioned, and I saw the girl's lips curl in disdain of her husband, and felt a trifle sad.

Another time (I have learnt since) Dick found them lunching together at Madarino's, a curious circumstance in view of the fact that she had said she was going to spend the day with her mother.

Then one afternoon Dick went home and sounded his motor-horn loudly as he swept up the drive, and discovered his wife at one end of the drawing-room and Steve at the other, and they were discussing Theosophy loudly.

After tea Dick linked his arm in Steve's and took him into the grounds.

"Steve, old boy," he said affectionately, "I don't think I should come and see Thelma unless somebody else is here, old man."

The Vampire of Wembley

"Why in Heaven's name shouldn't I?" asked Steve. "What rubbish you talk, Dick! Why, I've known Thelma as long as I've known you."

Dick scratched his chin.

"Yes, that seems a sound kind of argument," he said. "Still, I wouldn't if I were you. You know, servants and people of that kind talk."

But Steve smacked him on the back and told him not to be a goomp, and Thelma was so nice that evening that, when during a week-end Dick surprised his wife and Steve one morning walking with linked hands along an unfrequented path through the woods, he did no more than give them a cheery greeting, and passed on with a grin.

It was about this time that Dick started on his maladroit career. He became careless in his dress, could not move without knocking things over, went altogether wrong in his bridge, so that you could always tell which was Dick's score by a glance at the block. There was usually a monument of hundreds, two hundreds, and five hundreds erected above the line on the debit side, and when men cut him as a partner they groaned openly and frankly.

Harry Wallstein, who is a lunatic collector, gave him a rare Ming vase to examine, and Dick dropped it, smashing the delicate china into a hundred pieces. Of course he insisted upon paying the loss, but he could not soothe Harry's anguished soul. He had a trick too, when he was taking tea with some of his women friends, of turning quickly in a drawing-room and sweeping all the cups on to the floor. In the street he escaped death by miracles. Once he stood in the center of a crowded thoroughfare at the rush hour to admire the amethystine skies. A motor lorry and two taxicabs piled themselves up on the sidewalk in consequence, for it had been raining and the roads were slippery.

Dick footed the bill for the damage and went on his awkward way. It is extraordinary how quickly a man acquires a reputation for eccentricity. People forgot the unoffending Dick that used to be, and knew only the dangerous fool who was. When he called on Mrs. Tolmarsh, whose collection of Venetian glass has no equal in the country, the butler was instructed never to leave his side, to guide him in and out of the drawing-room, and under no circumstances to allow him to handle the specimens which Mrs. Tolmarsh invariably handed round for the admiration of her guests. Nevertheless he managed to crash a sixteenth-century vase and a decanter which had been made specially for Fillipo, Tyrant of Milan, and was adorned with his viperish crest.

And in the meantime Steven gave up his practice of calling three times a week on Mrs. Magnus and called every day.

Dick did not seem to mind, although he took to returning home earlier than had been his practice. I might have warned Dick. I preferred, however, to say a few words to Steven, and I got him alone in a corner of the library and I did not mince my words.

"I shall not moralize, Steven," I said, "for that is not my way. You have your own code and your own peculiar ideas concerning women, and so far you've got away with it. I do not doubt that you will get away with this matter because Dick seems to be drifting down the stream towards imbecility—but there are, thank Heaven, a few decent people in this town, and if you betray Dick you are going to have a pretty thin time. I won't commit the banality of asking you to look before you leap, because I know you're a pretty good looker!"

"Leaper!" he corrected. "No person who looks very carefully leaps at all. The world is divided into those two classes—lookers and leapers. Anyway, I am not very greatly concerned by what people think of me. If I were, I should have entered a monastery a long time ago. You've been straight with me, Doctor, and I'm going to be straight with you. My affairs are my affairs and concern nobody else. I shall do just as I think, and take a line which brings me the greatest satisfaction."

"Whosoever is hurt?" I asked.

"Whosoever is hurt," he said, and meant it. "I know just what is coming to me. I have figured it out."

There was no more to be said. To approach Dick was a much more delicate matter, for he was impervious to hints.

A week after I had talked to Steven I met Hariboy, who is a banker of standing and the president of my golf club. I met him professionally, for I had been called into his house to perform a minor operation on one of his children, and I was cleaning up in his dressing-room when he strolled in, and after some talk about the child he said:

"Steven Martingale is going away."

"Going away?" I repeated. "How do you know?"

"I know he has taken steamship accommodations for Bermuda. My secretary and his secretary are apparently friends, and she told my girl that Steven is doing a lot of rush work, and that he is leaving for a long holiday on the 18th."

"Do you know by what line?" I asked, and he told me.

Luckily the manager of the shipping office was a patient of mine, and I made it my business to call on him that afternoon.

"Yes, the ship leaves on the 18th," he said, "but I haven't Mr. Martingale on my passenger list."

We went through it together, and I traced my finger down the cabin numbers and their occupants.

"Who is this in No. 7 suite?" I asked. He put on his glasses and looked.

"Mr. and Mrs. Smith. I don't know who they are. It's not an uncommon name," he added humorously.

So that was that!

I do not think I should have moved any further in the matter if I had had the slightest degree of faith in Steven's honesty. But Steven was not a marrying man. He had once told me that under no circumstances would he think of binding his life with that of any woman, and had expounded his philosophy with that cold-blooded logic of his, which left me in no doubt at all that whatever fine promises he might make to Thelma Magnus, only one end of that advenlure was inevitable.

I sought Dick all over the town, and ran him to earth in the first place I should have looked—the card-room of Proctor's Club. I entered the room in time to hear the peroration of a violent address on idiocy delivered by Dick's late partner. His opponents were too busy adding up the score to take any interest in the proceeding.

Dick sat back in his chair, his hands in his pockets, a little smile on his thin face.

"Fortunes of war, old top," he murmured from time to time.

"Fortunes of war be—" roared Staine; who was his victim. "You go four spades on the queen, knave to five, and not another trick in your hand…!"

"Fortunes of war, old top," said Dick again, paid his opponents and rose, upsetting the table and scattering the cards in all directions.

"Awfully sorry," he murmured; "really awfully sorry!"

That "awfully sorry" of his came mechanically now.

"Now, Dick," said I, when I'd got him into my car, "you're coming straight home with me, and I'm going to talk to you like an uncle."

"Oh, Lord!" he groaned. "Not about Thelma?" I was astounded, and I suppose looked my astonishment. "Everybody talks to me about Thelma," said Dick calmly. "She's a dear, good girl, and as honest as they make 'em. I'm not a very amusing chap, you know, Doctor," he said mournfully, "and Steven is the kind of fellow who can keep a room in roars of laughter."

"But, my dear, good man," I said impatiently, "don't you realize that a man of Steven's character does not call daily on your wife to tell her funny stories?"

"I don't know," said Dick vaguely. "Thelma seems to like him, and I've really no grudge against old Steve. He's a leaper too," he said, with a quick, sidelong glance at me, "and that makes him ever so much more interesting to the women." lie chuckled at my astonishment. "He was telling us the other night about that amusing conversation he had with you."

"He did not tell you the whole of the conversation, I'll swear," said I dryly, but Dick showed no curiosity.

"Old Steven is a good fellow," he repeated. "I like him, and I tell everybody who comes to me with stories about him and Thelma that he is my very best friend."

I groaned in the spirit.

"Then," said I in despair, "it is useless telling you that Steven has booked two berths by the steamer which leaves on the 18th for Bermuda."

He nodded. "I know; he is taking his aunt," he said. "I got the same yarn from Chalmers, and I asked Steven, and he told me, yes, he was going away—"

"In the name of Smith?" I asked pointedly.

"In the name of Smith," repeated Dick gravely. "After all, he's a big power in the financial'world, Doctor, and it is not good business for him to advertise his comings and goings."

After that there was no more to be said.

"We're having a little party on the 17th at the house. I wish you would come along," said Dick before I left him. "I've particularly asked Steve to come. It will be a send-off for him, though of course nobody must know that he is going abroad."

The dear, simple fool said this so solemnly that I could have kicked him. What could I do? I had a talk with Chalmers, who is as fond of Dick as I am, and he could offer no advice.

"It's hopeless," he said, "and the queer thing is that Dick has arranged to go out of town on the night of the 17th. So we can't even drag him to the ship to confront this swine!"

"Do you think he'll marry her?" I asked after a long pause in the conversation.

"Marry her!" scoffed Chalmers. "Did he marry Fay Jennifer? Did he marry that unhappy girl Steele? Marry her!"

It was a big party which Dick gave. His house lay about twenty miles out of town and is situated in the most gorgeous country. It was a hot autumn day, with a cloudless sky and a warm gentle breeze, the kind of day that tempts even the most confirmed of city birds into the open country.

I do not think it was wholly the salubrious weather that was responsible for the big attendance. Half the people, and all the women who were present, knew that on the following day Steven Martingale was leaving for Bermuda, and that Thelma would accompany him.

I saw the girl as soon as I arrived, and noted the bright eyes, the flushed cheek, and the atmosphere of hectic excitement in which she moved. She was a little tremulous, somewhat incoherent, just a thought shrill.

All Dick's parties were amusing and just a little unconventional. For example, in addition to the band and the troupe of al fresco performers and Grecian dancers, he usually had some sort of competition for handsome prizes, and the young people, particularly, looked forward to these functions with the greatest enjoyment. On this occasion there was a revolver-shooting competition for ladies and gentlemen, the prize for the women being a diamond bangle, and for the men a gold cigarette case.

Most men imagine themselves to be proficient in the arts which they do not practice, and nine out of ten who have never handled a gun boast of their marksmanship.

Dick sought me out and took me into the house and upstairs to his own snuggery.

"Doctor," said he, as he dropped into an easychair and reached for his cigarettes, "spare a minute to enlighten me. What was the Crauford smash? I only heard a hint of it last night, and I'm told that dad was positively wonderful."

It was queer he had never heard of Ralph Crauford and his fall. Old Man Magnus and he were bitter enemies, and whereas Crauford must nag and splutter from day to day, Magnus was prepared to wait. As usual he laid his plans ahead, and one morning failed to turn up at his office. The rumor spread that he was ill, and there was suport for the story, because you could never pass his house without seeing a doctor's waiting car. It was a puzzling case, and I myself was fooled. So was every specialist we brought in. For weeks at a time Magnus would be well, and then he would have a collapse and be absent from his office for days.

And all the time the Crauford crowd were waiting to jump in and smash two of the stocks he carried. We had advised a trip abroad, but it was not till the end of a year of these relapses and recoveries that he consented. He went to Palermo in Sicily, and after a month it was announced that he had died. Then the fun started. Crauford jumped into the market with a hammer in each hand, figuratively speaking. Tyne River Silver fell from 72 to 31, and all the time the executors of the estate were chasing one another to discover their authority to act. This went on for three days and then the blow fell. Old Man Magnus appeared on 'Change, looking a trifle stouter, a little browner, and infinitely cheerful.

Crauford had "sold over." It cost him his bank balance, his town house, and his country estate plus his wife's jewelry to get square with Magnus.

Dick listened to the story, his eyes beaming, interrupting me now and again with a chuckle of sheer joy.

"Wonderful old dad!" he said at the end; "wonderful old boy! And he was foxing all the time. Kidding 'em along! The art of it, the consummate art of it! Specialists and sea voyages and bulletins every hour!"

He stood up abruptly and threw away his cigarette.

"Let's go and see the women shoot," he said.

There was the usual fooling amongst the girls when their end of the competition started. In spite of their "Which-end-shall-I- hold-it?" and their mock terror, they shot remarkably well.

I had caught a glimpse of Steven, a silent, watchful, slightly amused man, who most conspicuously avoided Thelma, but came down to the booth and stood behind her when she fired her six shots for the prize. Incidentally not one bullet touched the target, and the wobbling of her pistol was pitiful.

Steven's shooting was beautiful to watch. Every bullet went home in the center of the target and the prize was assuredly his.

"Now watch me, Steve," said Dick, and at the sight of Dick with a gun in his hand even his best friends drew back.

He fired one shot, a bull's-eye, the second shot was a little bit to the left, but nevertheless a bull's-eye, the third shot passed through the hole which the first had made, the fourth and fifth were on the rim of the black center—and then he turned with a smile to Steven.

"My old pistol is much better than the best of the new ones," he said.

He had refused to shoot with the weapons provided, and had brought a long ungainly thing of ancient make; but as he was not a competitor in the strict sense of the word, there had been no protest.

The sixth shot went through the bull and there was a general clapping.

"How's that?" said Dick, twiddling his revolver.

"Fine," said Steven. "The Looker shoots almost as well as the Leaper," laughed Dick, and pressed the trigger carelessly. There was a shot and a scream. Steve balanced himself for a moment, looking at Dick in a kind of awed amazement, and then crumpled up and fell.

As for Dick he stood, the smoking revolver still in his hand, frowning down at the prostrate figure.

"I'm sorry," he muttered, but Steven Martingale had passed beyond the consideration of apologies. He was dead before I could reach him.

*

That old-fashioned revolver of Dick's had seven chambers, and people agreed both before and after the inquest that it was the kind of fool thing that Dick would have.

"He ought to have seen there were seven shots when he loaded the infernal weapon," said Chalmers. "Of course, if it was anybody but Dick I should have thought that the whole thing was manoeuvred, and that all this awkwardness of his had been carefully acted for twelve months in order to supply an excuse at the inquest and get the 'Accidental Death' verdict. It is the sort of thing that his father would have done. A keen, far-seeing old devil was John Magnus."

I said nothing, for I had seen the look in Dick's eyes when he said "leaper."

At any rate, the shock wakened Dick, for his awkwardness fell away from him like an old cloak, and Thelma Magnus must have found some qualities in him which she had not suspected, for she struck me as a tolerably happy woman when I met her the other day. But I shall not readily forget that hard glint in Dick's eyes when he spoke the last words which Steven Martingale was destined to hear. I had seen it once before in the eyes of John Seymour Magnus the day he smashed Crauford.

Maybe some of the old man's hormones were working. I should like to ask Foley about it.

The Vampire of Wembley

The Speed Test

MISS JANE IDA MEAGH was prepared to brain the first misguided person who addressed her by either of her given names, and had accepted with gratitude at a very early age the appellation suggested by the combination of her initials—Jim. And from "Jim" to "Jimmy" is but a short step.

In the census return Jimmy described herself as a "stenographer." So might Edison have marked himself "electrician" or Napoleon "soldier." For there was no stenographer like Jimmy. She was at the very head of her profession, and was booked ahead like a film-star or a Harley Street specialist.

If there was one person in the world whom Jimmy hated and loathed with all her soul, that person was Henry Obbings. Henry was a limp youth who gave you the impression that he had shaved in a bad light. He was famous in the social circle in which he moved for his ready wit and a gift of repartee. He invariably recounted with a wealth of detail his encounters with Jimmy, and repeated with great effect the things he had said to Jimmy on these occasions.

It is true that the majority of his pert replies were those he remembered long after he had left Jimmy, and it is also a fact that he never quite gave a faithful account of what Jimmy had said to him. There were some things which Henry could never bring himself to repeat.

Henry Obbings was the pet speedster of the Rat-a-plan Typewriter Co. Ltd., and from time to time there were issued by him or on his behalf challenges to the whole of civilised mankind, man or woman, to meet him in a speed contest, the only conditions being that Mr. Obbings should operate on a Number 6 Silent Rat-a-plan, "the writer that writes."

For the purpose of this challenge Jimmy regarded herself as inhuman; she steadfastly and resolutely declined to beat Mr. Obbings privately or publicly, and sneered openly at Mr. Obbings's portrait in the newspapers. These appeared from time to time, for the Rat-a-plan had an excellent Press agent, and they revealed Mr. Obbings working at his machine, a sycophantic attendant standing by with an oil-can. It was a legend that he worked so fast that after half-an-hour's use the bearings of the machine became so hot that it was necessary to open the door and windows of the room in which he worked, to let the temperature cool down.

There were also pictures of Mr. Obbings in his moments of leisure and recreation, sitting at a table, with his head upon his clenched fists, looking at a book with a studious, even sad expression.

One morning there came to Jimmy a further challenge by Mr. Henry Obbings. There was an annual exhibition at which business appliances of all kinds were shown, and it was a feature of this event that a diploma and a gold medal were competed for by stenographers. So far it had resulted in a walk-over for Henry.

Jimmy had turned down every such artful move and invitation, and she now dropped the letter into her waste-paper basket with an exaggerated gesture of disgust. Nor did the information that the Rat-a-plan Typewriter Co. offered an additional money prize of substantial value to anyone who could exceed the speed of Mr. Obbings produce a trace of irresolution to her decision.

She got up from her breakfast-table briskly and looked at her engagement-book. Jimmy was booked ahead, as has been remarked before, like a fashionable physician. Her amazing quickness, her accuracy, her unquestionable integrity justified the big fees she received, and incidentally confirmed her wisdom when she set out to be a specialist stenographer.

Her first call that day was on Dr. John Phillips, who was also a specialist in his way; and Dr. John, who looked a little tired under the eyes, as well he might be, for he had been up all night with a dying patient, received her at his morning meal.

"Thanks, no, doctor," said Jimmy. "I've just breakfasted."

"This is my supper," growled the doctor. "Jimmy, I've the details of fourteen cases to dictate to you, and I hope you feel fitter for the job than I. By the way," he said curiously, "where did you get your extraordinary knowledge from? You've never yet spelt a medical term wrongly."

"I got them out of a book, the same as you," said Jimmy.

The doctor looked at her admiringly.

The Vampire of Wembley

For the next hour and a quarter she was absorbed in the gruesome and sorrowful business of recording the histories of cases, every other one of which ended: "The patient died at 11.45," or whatever the hour might have been.

"Don't any of your patients get well?" asked Jimmy as she snapped the band round her note-book.

"Just a few," said Phillips. "Don't forget, I'm only called in at the very end in lots of cases. I think some of them expect me to bring my trumpet, under the impression that I am the Archangel Gabriel."

"A rotten life!" said Jimmy thoughtfully. "I'd sooner have my job."

The doctor looked at his watch.

"I must hurry. I've got to go to Greenwich," he said.

Nevertheless, and in spite of his hurry, he sat down again at his desk and lit a cigarette, offering one to Jimmy, who shared a common match.

"Jimmy, do you think that a young man with brilliant prospects, but no money, should marry a very nice girl and start family life on—that!" He snapped his fingers to indicate a microscopic income.

"It all depends upon the prospects," said Jimmy cautiously. "If there's only a prospect of raising a largo family, I should say no."

"And I said no, too," said the specialist with a sigh.

He was a youngish man, remembering the position he occupied in the medical world, and that he could still sigh over the follies of his fellow-men was a wholesome tribute to his youth.

"He's a pal of mine. We were at University together," he said.

Jimmy guessed that the unknown He was the patient at Greenwich. Dr. John was looking at the ceiling thoughtfully.

"I was talking to him about you yesterday."

"About me?" said Jimmy in surprise.

"Yes, about you. I don't think he has a great deal of money—in fact I know he hasn't," said Phillips frankly, "and it's hard luck that at a time when he's really ill—he's had a bad nervous breakdown—he should have had a good offer from one of the technical journals for a series of articles."

He paused and blew a ring of smoke to the rafters.

"Jimmy, I know your fees, and they are beautifully exorbitant. God bless you for keeping the specialist beyond the reach of common people. But if he asks you to go down—for I think he could dictate these articles; he certainly could not write them—I wish you'd charge him a sum which is not ridiculously low, but which is not your ordinary rate. One minute," he said as she was going to speak. "I want you to put the rest of your fee on my bill."

"I'll do nothing of the kind, doctor," said Jimmy quietly. "I'd do this job for nothing, but I suppose he wouldn't like that. Anyhow, I'll do it at an ordinary typist's fee, and as to putting the rest of the charge on your account, that's ridiculous, unless you send me a bill for doctoring my throat last spring and for giving me several helpful pieces of advice about my heart, lungs, and other important parts of me."

He laughed as he rose.

"I must go, Jimmy. I'll let you know about Fennell."

*

THAT morning Miss Jane Ida Meagh was the victim of a trick. She had been engaged by a firm of manufacturer's agents to copy a long document dealing with the cork harvest of Spain. She had to do the work at the agent's office, and it was urged upon her that it was vital, was indeed a matter of life and death that she should get to the last word of that report in the briefest possible space of time.

It was a brand new typewriter, of a brand new make, at which she sat. The keyboard was, of course, universal, and most of the gadgets were of a type with which she was unfamiliar, though their manipulation was very easily learnt.

She had fixed the tension to her liking, and then—the machine grew eloquent under her lightning fingers.

"There's your report," she said, and observed that the agent had a stop watch in his hand.

"Five thousand words in forty-two minutes 15.2 seconds," he said breathlessly but exactly.

"I dare say," said Jimmy. "Shall I send you a bill or are you one of those never-owe-nobody people?"

The agent for this occasion was of the latter variety. Jimmy collected her cheque and left, and there the incident appeared to have closed.

But the next day she passed a shop window in which was a typewriter. And beneath the typewriter was a large sign:

THE PLATEN TYPEWRITER
on which
MISS JANE IDA MEAGH
(the world's champion stenographer)
wrote 5,347 words in 42 min. 15.2 secs.
A Record For The World.
Come Inside and Look at This
New Marvel of Engineering Science:
"THE MACHINE WITH A MIND."

"God bless my soul!" said Jimmy, and despite this pious invocation went red with wrath.

She swept into the shop and demanded to see the manager.

"Take my name out of your window," she said peremptorily when that gentleman made his appearance.

"But, my dear young lady—"

"Take it out or I'll sue you for libel," she said. "Anyway, it's a lie. I took an hour and a quarter to do the work, on the worst brand of machine that I've ever handled. And what's more, I shall make an affidavit to that effect."

"It's a good machine," he protested; "there are only three in existence; they're show samples, and—"

"Three too many!" snapped Jimmy.

"Mr. Brown said—

If Brown is the nom-de-guerre of the Armenian who engaged me to copy the cork serial," said Jimmy, "I don't want to hear what he said. Now, do you take out that placard, or do I tell the Press all my troubles?"

"I'll take it out," growled the manager. "I must say, though, that you're not very considerate. You'll remember that I gave you a lot of work last summer—"

"You can give it to somebody else next summer," retorted Jimmy promptly. "Perhaps she'll do it on 'The Platen.' It's a fairly good machine for two-finger typists. Try 'em with 'Now is the time for all good men to come to the aid of the party'!"

She fired this invitation as she left him, and there was a sting in it which only a real typist will understand.

The placard was removed, and there the matter would have ended, for Jimmy was discretion itself, and she was in no mood to advertise the trick that had been played upon her. What annoyed her most was that the machine was really good and a distinct improvement on any she had ever used.

Unfortunately, the manager was not so discreet, and the news came to a wandering reporter. The reporter, who was a clever young reporter, wrote a most amusing story that covered the Platen Typewriter, without mentioning its title, with shame and ignominy, so that in every office where girls groped for keys and dreamt dreams of making Miss Jane Ida Meagh look like a pickled walnut, the Platen Typewriter became synonymous with foolishness.

The publicity had the effect of spurring Mr. Henry Obbings to a further challenge, to whom Jimmy was stung to a reply:

Dear Sir,

You ask me whether I will make on exhibition of myself, and urge as a reason the fact that you intend making an exhibition of yourself. The only inducement I can see for me so far forgetting myself is the paragraph in which you tell me that I should work at one end of the building and you at the other. The knowledge that we were as far apart as possible would be an inducement were it not for the fact that the certainty that I was under the same roof as yourself would make me sick.

The Vampire of Wembley

Yours sincerely,
J. I. Meagh.

It was a very rude letter, such a letter as Mr. Obbings explained to his friends, no lady would write. Possibly he was justified.

"The truth is," said Mr. Obbings... "no, Percy, I won't show you the letter, it's too disgraceful for words—the fact is she knows jolly well I could lick the stuffing out of her in spite of her vaunted speed."

Yes, Mr. Obbings used the words "vaunted speed."

"Perhaps she'll enter at the last minute?" suggested the friend.

"I'm afraid not." Mr. Obbings shook his head with the sad smile of a tiger deprived of a meal.

*

A FEW days later Jimmy was rung up on the 'phone. It was Dr. Phillips.

"Can you go down there to-day, Jimmy?" he asked. "Fennell thinks he could dictate the article, and he has got together most of the data."

"I'm free this afternoon," said Jimmy.

"I'll wire that you're coming then. Be there at half-past two," said the doctor, and gave her the address.

That morning Jimmy had a great idea. Here was an invalid. She did not know much about invalids except that they lay in bed and refused delicate food. Sometimes they nibbled at a grape or swallowed a mouthful of chocolates, but now and again by a miracle they could be tempted to negotiate some particularly appetising dish, whereafter they put on weight and recovered with the greatest rapidity.

That morning Jimmy stood in her private kitchen, her sleeves rolled up, a cookery-book propped against a milk-bottle, and the light of battle in her eye.

No man or woman knew her ghastly secret. Even Mr. Obbings in his wildest moments never dreamt that her vice was the mangling and cremation of flour and fruit. Her lips moved as she followed the directions in the book.

"Flour, two spoonfuls.... Fresh butter... put in a dry, warm place... bake in a slow oven...."

90

She drew a long sigh and switched on her electric oven. She ate a hurried lunch, dashing backward and forward to the kitchen to examine the little thermostat which regulated the heat of the oven, and to compare the watch which lay open on the dresser with a note of the minute and the second that her work had gone to a warmer climate, written in pencil on the edge of the cookery-book.

She opened the oven, and with a cloth drew out the steel plate on which four beautiful confections lay, and the fragrance of them was as incense to her nostrils.

She looked at her work, then opened the cookery-book and examined the coloured plates, on which was a life-like representation of the little cakes she was baking. They were exact! If anything her creations were an improvement upon the book. She bore them to her room, and on her face was a look of holy exaltation. Each one she wrapped in white tissue and packed them into a small box and put the box into her attaché case.

She arrived at Greenwich in the afternoon. The Fennell's house was a small one and poorly furnished, she saw at a glance.

A girl met her at the door, a smiling bright-eyed girl who had laughed at poverty so long that it had become a habit.

"You're Miss Meagh, aren't you?" she said. "It is very good of you to come so far."

Jimmy, who was somewhat at sea on occasions like this, smiled and was glad to get an awkward situation over. She found her client lying on a sofa in a somewhat bare parlour. He was a man of thirty, and he looked terribly ill, Jimmy thought. A low table near by was piled high with books, newspaper cuttings, and blue-covered reports.

"My husband has been ill," explained Mrs. Fennell. "But he's much better now, aren't you, Frank?"

"Oh, much! I'm just loafing now," said the man with a grin. "I think I can dictate the best part of the article this afternoon, Miss Meagh."

"Fire away," said Jimmy, and produced her book.

Fennell's estimate of his strength had erred on the optimistic side. After three-quarters of an hour of dictation he was exhausted.

"I'm sorry," he said ruefully. "I thought I was stronger."

"Don't worry," said Jimmy. "You've dictated quite a lot. Anyway, I can come down to-morrow afternoon."

"It's a long way out of town," he said doubtfully.

"Rubbish!" said Jimmy, and that settled the matter.

They pressed her to stay to tea, and she needed very little pressing. She had not had the opportunity she had sought, and as tea was to be served in the drawing-room she thought that this was a chance not to be missed. In the interval of waiting she was introduced to the Fennell baby, and as usual, when babies swam into her ken, she became incoherent and foolish.

"I always get maudlin over babies," she said apologetically. "Of course, it is every girl's pose that she loves them, but I'm honest. I admit it."

The maid brought in the tea, a plate of bread and butter, some jam sandwiches, and a large sponge-cake. Jimmy waited breathlessly.

"No, thanks, dear, I won't eat anything," said Mr. Fennell with a little shiver as he ran his eyes over the meal. "No, thank you," he said again as though he had asked himself and refused.

"Really, you ought to eat something, Frank," said his pretty wife, looking concerned.

Jimmy coughed. "A friend of mine makes rather good pastries," she said carelessly. "She's rather a good cook, and curiously enough she sent me..."

She opened her attaché case and took out the box with fingers which shook a little.

Would they have retained their beautiful shape and appearance? Before now Jimmy had known the most remarkable changes to occur between oven and eating. She removed the wrappings from one with a reverent touch. It was as it had been! Fennell's eyes fastened upon it.

"That does look good!" He reached out his hand. "Have you one to spare?" He took the pastry between his finger and thumb and bit into it.

Jimmy held her breath and half closed her eyes.

"Splendid!" he said. "This is the most wonderful thing I've had for years."

"Would you like one, Mrs. Fennell?" asked Jimmy in a hollow voice. Her heart was thumping. She could have wept at that moment.

"Really, it's so extraordinary to see Frank eat that I can hardly take my eyes from him," laughed Mrs. Fennell.

She nibbled at the cake.

"It's really delicious. Your friend must be very clever."

"Oh, very!" said Jimmy huskily. "Perhaps she will send me some more to-morrow."

"Aren't you eating any yourself?" asked Fennell.

"No," said Jimmy eagerly, and fumbled for the other two. "Would you like them?"

Mr. Fennell not only liked them, but he ate them. He, an invalid, who had refused the choicest productions of the O.K. Cake Company (or the label about the sponge-cake lied), was eating with every evidence of relish the creature of her brain and hand.

"You can come to-morrow, can you?" asked Mrs. Fennell.

"I can come," said Jimmy, speaking under stress of great emotion, "if—if you want me."

It was a lame conclusion. The conversation drifted away from cakes, and Mrs. Fennell took the girl into her confidence.

"We've had a lot of bad luck, haven't we, Frank?"

"Just a little," ho said.

"Do you know that a week ago I thought we were going to be quite wealthy," the girl went on. "Frank is an inventor, and he has invented one of the best typewriters that has ever been put on the market, and just fancy, because some stupid girl refused to work it, the manufacturers turned it down!"

"I think she was right," said Fennell. "Apparently they got her to do a speed test by means of a trick, and they rather over-reached themselves."

"They were going to give Frank a big sum of money on account of royalties, but now we hear that a lot of orders, which had been booked, have been cancelled."

The Vampire of Wembley

Jane Ida Meagh did not swoon. She sat up straight and stared at the girl-wife.

"What was the name of that machine?" she asked faintly.

"I called it 'The Platen,' because the . . ." He explained why it was called "The Platen," but Jimmy did not hear.

She had ruined them—these lovely people of taste and refinement! This poor man stretched upon a bed of sickness! Jimmy's eyes filled with tears, and she gulped at the extravagant picture of misery she drew. She had done it! And from sheer caprice and femininity. Jimmy had always hated femininity, and now it seemed the most loathsome of weaknesses.

"You'll come to-morrow, and don't forget those cakes," said Mrs. Fennell.

*

JIMMY went on the next day, and the cakes she took were even more delicious than the last, for she had mercifully refrained from improving upon the recipe—which was occasionally Jimmy's super-weakness.

That evening on her return to town she went into the shop where the "Platen" had been exhibited, and the manager, standing with his hands behind him in the middle of the floor space, greeted her with a grave but reserved nod.

"Good afternoon, Miss Meagh," he said.

"Good afternoon, Mr. Salter," for that was the manager's name.

"How is the trade in 'Platens'?" asked Jimmy briskly.

"Well, you smashed that for us," said Mr. Salter bitterly. "But, still, I don't mind so much, because I am thinking of taking over the Rat-a-plan agency for their improved portable machine."

"Don't do it," said Jimmy. "What are you charging for the 'Platen'?"

He named the price, and she produced her cheque-book.

"You're not going to buy a machine?" he cried in amazement.

"There are two other ways I can get one," said Jimmy. "One is by stealing it, and the other by accepting it as a gift—both of which methods are objectionable to me."

"But you're—"

"Get that flat-footed boy of yours to carry this to my cab, will you? I'm not so strong as I was twenty years ago." Which was true, for Jimmy's age was twenty-four.

The flat-footed boy, who was now a scowling flat-footed boy, carried the instrument to the waiting taxi, and Jimmy placed it on her table that night with determination in the set of her jaw, and the light of battle in her eye.

*

MR. HENRY OBBINGS sat in a gaily-decorated stand, surrounded by a large crowd of admiring stenographers, and demonstrated, what time a smooth and silky-voiced lecturer dilated upon the staggering qualities of the Rat-a-plan.

"Un-for-tun-ate-ly," he said, "we have not the op-por-tun-ity of test-ing the rela-tive speed of the Rat-a-plan with any of its com-pet-i-tors." He spoke as though each syllable was separated from its fellow. "Our challenge extended to the whole of the civilised world has not been accepted by any of our rivals, for reasons which I think need no explanation. Tonight, we had hoped there would be a competition for the Inter-Trades Diploma and Medal, together with the money prize offered by my company, but you are deprived of that interesting demonstration. As you will see, we are the only entrants in the competition."

He pointed to a large bulletin board where the name of "Mr. Henry Obbings, The Rat-a-plan Typewriter," was visible.

It was at that moment that the secretary of the exhibition pinned beneath the notice:

"J. I. Meagh, The Platen Typewriter."

THE contest will remain in the minds of all interested in the delicate art of stenography. The two competitors sat, not at either end of the building, but at the same bench, each with the matter to be copied neatly stacked on their left and a pile of virgin white paper as neatly stacked on their right, and at the word "Go!" both struck simultaneously at the keys.

The Vampire of Wembley

The test was for half-an-hour's continuous work, and in that thirty minutes Jimmy wrote 4,630 words without a mistake, beating the baffled Henry Obbings by exactly twelve hundred words.

Incidentally, she established the name of the Platen Typewriter, so that to-day there is scarcely an office in the City where the peculiar tick-tick of its keys cannot be heard.

The Junior Reporter

IF the junior reporter approached the platform with awe and reverence, it was because he was the junior reporter.

You must understand that Sir Thomas was in the chair, and Mr. Hilldry (Lord of the Manor) was prominently displayed in the front row of the platform.

Miss Cicily was there, too—they say down at Taunborough that she has half-a-million in her own right—and the canon and goodness knows what other celebrities.

The junior reporter, who was born and bred in Taunborough, looked round the crowded audience, and his heart swelled with pride that Taunborough had risen to the occasion; that Taunborough had been worthy of itself; and it may be that in this his melting mood a youthful tear glistened in his eye. He rather hoped that Sir Thomas would recognise him, but somehow Sir Thomas had no eyes for the line of young men that sat at the reporters' table sharpening their pencils.

Naturally enough, with Mr. Hilldry contesting the seat, rendered vacant by the retirement of his brother, local feeling ran high. Indeed, the junior reporter, telegraphing to his newspaper at Bristol, had said so in exactly those words. Naturally, too, the junior reporter reflected that shade of political opinion so ably represented by Mr. Hilldry.

Because it was an important by-election, there were reporters from London and from Plymouth, and between a Londoner and weary Devonian the junior reporter found himself.

They were both very pleasant young men, especially he who came from

London. He had a shock of hair and wore pince-nez, and before Sir Thomas rose to open the meeting he leant across to his colleague from Devonshire and asked:

"What's it worth?"

"This?" said the Devonshire man, sharpening his pencil. "Oh, about a short half for us."

"Two sticks for us," grumbled the gentleman from town, "unless," he added, hopefully, "there's a riot."

"There'll be no riot," said the other contemptuously, "Taunborough's the slowest place on earth!"

The junior reporter listened resentfully; for his part, so far from a "short half," this meeting would be recorded in five closely-set columns.

"Who's Sir Thomas?" asked the London man.

The junior reporter would have been delighted to volunteer the necessary information, but the Devon man anticipated him.

"Oh, Sir Thomas," he said offhandedly, just as though he'd been discussing some ordinary man, "is a local person, a little tin god in his way—he'll bore your head off."

The junior gasped.

"If he speaks for an hour," the Devon man went on gloomily, "there won't be two lines you can report; but perhaps," he reflected, "he won't speak."

"What is the candidate like?"

"Shocking," said the Devon man frankly.

The junior reporter found his voice.

"Perhaps, gentlemen," he said with elaborate sarcasm, "the candidate's views do not coincide with yours."

The London man regarded him curiously.

"Speaking for myself, they don't," he confessed. "That is partly because I have no views; so far as the political colour of my paper is concerned, we are red-hot supporters of the candidate."

"Politics," said the Devonshire oracle, "means one set of rotters trying to chuck another set of rotters out—"

The Vampire of Wembley

"Ladies and gentlemen..." (Roars of cheering).

Sir Thomas was on his feet, and the junior reporter poised his pencil over virgin pad.

"Ladies and gentlemen. I am sure—I am quite sure that you do not expect me, that you are not expecting a speech, a long speech from me tonight, this evening. We all know, most of us know, in fact we all know, we are all well acquainted with our friend and neighbour Mr. Hilldry Simes-Patrick. (Cheers.) I've known him, that is, I remember him when he was a little boy, quite a small boy in frocks. (Laughter.) I remember his father...."

"He's started," groaned the gentleman from Devonshire.

A sibilant whisper ran along the reporters' table.

"Somebody wants you," said the Devon man, and the Londoner leant forward and looked down the table.

"You taking this?" asked the whisperer hoarsely.

"No," said the London man.

"Good," said the whisperer, "I was afraid you were—how long will he talk...."

Sir Thomas had stopped speaking and was glaring at the audience.

A thin old man with big gig-lamp spectacles on his nose, and clutching a bundle of notes, was standing up, to the indignation of his scandalised neighbours.

"... I would like to ask Sir Thomas," he piped.

"I cannot answer you—wait until I have finished my speech," said Sir Thomas, very red in the face.

"... Will you explain the attitood of Mr. Chamberlain in the year 1875, when he said...."

"Sit down! Sit down, sir!"

"... Speakin' at the town 'all Birmingham on March 10th he referred to the dooty of the proletariat...."

No man cried "Sit down!" more fiercely than did the junior reporter; no partisan applauded Sir Thomas more vigorously, and certainly no journalist took so complete and copious a note of the great man's speech as did that representative of the press.

"A quarter of an hour," said the Devon man gratefully, when the chairman resumed his seat amidst loud and continued cheering. (I quote again from the script of the junior reporter.)

A burst of wild cheering: "For he's a jolly good feller" in several keys, and a smiling figure at the chairman's table.

"This," said the London man, apprehensively, "is, I presume, His Nibs!"

"That's him," said young Devonshire, ungrammatically.

Those excerpts I have been able to take from the junior reporter's book enable me to fit in the speech—as I heard it.

"... the pendulum has swung back, and the pendulum has swung true."

"A little bit mixed up in his metaphor," said the Devonshire reporter.

The junior, who thought the figure of speech beautifully apt, scowled.

"... We are going forward to a winning cause, the goal is in sight and we will not turn back—(cheers)—the prosperity of the country is in the hands of the people, let there be no...."

"What did he say after 'people,'?" asked the London man.

"I don't know," said the Devon man in despair. "Whatever he said doesn't matter much."

The junior reporter could have told them, but he spitefully covered the passage "let there be no wavering in the ranks of progress" with the palm of his hand.

The gentleman from London ran his fingers through his hair wearily.

"There were three jobs I might have taken," he said deliberately. "I might have done a memorial service, or the opening of the Oyster Fishery Exhibition, or the Brixton murder; and to think," he soliloquised bitterly, "to think that I chose this!"

"... whatever might be the opinion of a few self-seeking politicians with axes to grind—(cheers)—the vast majority of the electorate is in favour of...."

"I rather like funerals," mused the Devon man, "you get such a splendid opportunity of ringing the changes on 'sombre magnificence' and 'gloomy grandeur'—why didn't you take the memorial service?"

The London man yawned and shook his head wearily.

"... we cannot put back the clock—(cheers)—we cannot—er—identify ourselves with an anachronism...."

The junior reporter, with a rapt frown, scribbled down the burning words, faithfully, religiously, literally.

"....if you send me to the House of Commons—"

Above the speaker's monotonous voice rose a shrill cry. A cry that sent an indignant flush to the junior reporter's cheek, that brought a bright light to the eye of the London man, that jerked a dozen bored metropolitan journalists to their feet seeking the face of the interrupting member of the audience.

Again the thin voice.

"Votes for wimmin!"

"Madam," muttered the London man under his breath, as the uproar began, "from the bottom of my heart I thank you!"

"So" (I quote the junior reporter again) "the meeting concluded in great disorder, owing to the unseemly conduct of two ladies." And after "ladies" the junior reporter put marks like this: (?), but his all-wise editor cut them out.

If—?

THE war had soured Hector Smith. It had drawn a line between comparative youth and comparative middle-age. It had burst inconveniently, as wars have a habit of bursting, upon more than one half-matured scheme of his, and had scattered them to bits and left him the poorer. To be exact, it had left Mary the poorer, because it was Mary's money that went, of which fact it had become a habit of hers to remind him.

But more souring, bits of boys, the merest urchins, to be patronized or ignored in the old days, had obtruded themselves upon his and the public's attentions. The balance of life was over-set. The inconsiderable factors (in which category he included these boys who now strutted consciously be-ribboned through his world) had grown to such importance that they overshadowed the real big things of life, such as his handicap at golf, his bridge hands, the remarkable poverty of intelligence on the part of his partners, and the like.

There was a time when Arthur, for example, would have been carried to the seventh heaven by a timely half-sovereign, and would have run his long legs off in his haste to reach the confectioner's before the cream buns were sold. Now Arthur was a straight-limbed youth with "wings," and a record of good service in France.

And Arthur and Mary—

Pshaw! It was absurd! Why, he remembered this dirty little kid when he was so high! Yet, it was a fact that Mary spent most of her time with Arthur, raved about his dancing, his beautiful manners, his perfect sympathy. Pshaw!

Hector Smith cursed the war that forced him to listen to gruesome stories in which he was not interested.

He opened the drawing-room door and stalked in, then stopped with a little grimace. The inevitable Arthur was there, and the inevitable Arthur with an embarrassed giggle made his escape with a mumbled reference to the weather. As for Mary, she looked too good to be true.

"Hasn't that bird got a perch of his own?" snarled Hector.

"How can you speak of a man who has been wounded—?" began his indignant partner.

Mr. Smith laughed contemptuously.

"Wounded! The first time he tried to fly he crashed, and the second time he tried to fly he crashed, and the third time he tried to fly he crashed!"

She tossed her head.

"I'd like to see you do it!"

Mr. Smith shrugged.

"Oh, I know it's a mistake to talk disrespectfully of your hero," he sneered. He was not feeling at his brightest.

"What do you mean?" she demanded with ominous calm.

"I mean, I'm fed up, that's what I mean," he snapped, and she flamed round on him.

The Vampire of Wembley

"And so am I!" she cried. "You're vulgar and stupid and tyrannical. The life I've lived with you is abominable. When I married you I had money—"

He bowed.

"That's right," he said, encouragingly, "throw that in my face! Didn't I invest it for you?" It was an unfortunate question.

"Yes, you did," she said, bitterly. "You put it into a luminous sign business. Luminous signs! And a month after war was declared! And the only thing you could get out of showing a luminous sign was six months' imprisonment!"

"How did I know there was going to be a war?" asked the exasperated man.

"You might have guessed it," she replied, illogically.

"Could I guess that London was to be plunged in darkness? I did my best. I should have made a million out of that fuse factory I started this year—"

"Yes, if it hadn't been for the armistice," she scoffed.

"How did I know there was going to be peace?" he roared.

She flounced past him on her way to the door.

"Oh, you never know anything!"

"There's one thing I know," he shouted after her.

"What's that?"

"One of these fine days I'll run away to America!" Her scornful laugh came back through the slammed door. He threw himself upon the settee. The money was gone and the wife remained. That was his luck. If it had been the other way about—! If only it had been the other way about! If he could only live the years over again! If he could only be five years younger and knew what he knew!

He sat staring at the newspaper in his hand. There was a critique of a new play, a fairy play.

Bah! Fairies were nonsense!

He laid the newspaper down on his knees.

But suppose there were such things as fairies, and suppose they moved about this prosaic, industrialized world as in the old days they moved through the woodland glebes; suppose by a wave of a magic wand a man could be

102

transplanted back, back, back; and suppose that it were possible that the clock should be put back, and one had consciousness of all the things that were going to happen, the horses that were going to win races, the stocks which were going to rise, all the great events which must occur!

He heaved a deep sigh and looked up. He half-rose from the couch, for there before him, a bright and radiant figure in the dusky room, stood a brilliant presence. He knew it was a fairy because it was dressed as fairies should be dressed, and bemuse she was bathed in a flood of silvery light which seemed to come from nowhere in particular. The little hands grasped a wand which twinkled and glittered with light.

Recovering from his initial astonishment he looked at her aappraisingly. He felt it would be undignified and ill-bred to regard her as a phenomenon.

"Hector Smith," said a sweet, low voice,

"I am your fairy godmother!"

"Oh, yes." said Hector Smith, politely.

"You have expressed a wish to be five years younger. Be happy, for to-morrow you will awake in 1914."

"Eh?" said Hector, sitting up. "I say, do you really mean that?"

She inclined her head.

"Wait a moment," said Hector, eagerly. "I must be the only one who knows it. D'ye understand? Because if everybody else knows it I shall be in the cart again."

She raised her wand and waved it slowly above his head.

"I must be the only one who knows that there's going to be a war and all that sort of thing," said Hector, drowsily. A sense of languor was rapidly overcoming him. "I don't want...."

His head fell on his chest.

He did not know how long he had slept when he awoke with a jerk. He had a confused dream in which figured fairies and brilliant wands, and low, sweet voices mingled, and then he remembered that he had to see Tomkins who was liquidating his ill-fated fuse factory. He went to the study and 'phoned Tomkins, but, amazingly enough, Tomkins was not on the 'phone. He asked

Exchange to connect him with Smith's Patent Fuse Factory, but Exchange was ignorant that such a place had ever existed.

"The telephone service," said Hector Smith, as be hung up the receiver, "is becoming more and more abominable."

He decided to write to the newspapers on the subject. He paused outside the drawing-room door, for he heard his wife moving about inside, and it was necessary to brace himself up for the ordeal. He was a little scared of Mary in her tantrums, and more scared that his apprehension should be known to her. But the girl who came across the room to meet him had no frown, no reproaches. She was one beaming smile, and she ran towards him and laid her hands upon his shoulders.

"Dearie!" she kissed him, ecstatically: then noting the gloom in his face, "darling, whatever is the matter?"

"Matter?" he answered, suspiciously. "What's that you did? What's the matter with you?"

She looked at him in wonder.

"Nothing is the matter with me. I just kissed you, that's all."

He heaved a sigh. How did she know he had received his directors' cheque that day?

"How much do you want?" he asked, with resignation.

"Naughty boy, why do you say that?" she pouted. "Don't you love your diddlelums any more?"

He stared at her.

"Look here. What's up?" he asked, desperately. "I'll buy it! What's wrong with you?"

"Wrong?"

She was frankly astonished.

"Everything has gone wrong to-day," he growled. "I went to call up that fellow about the fuses—"

She frowned.

"Fuses? What are fuses?"

His suspicions returned. "Don't pull my leg," he said, coldly. "I'm not in a mood for it. Try it on the other fellow."

"What other-fellow?" He jerked his head to the door.

"He was heme just now. I heard his voice."

A smile of understanding dawned on her face.

"Who, little Arthur?"

"Yes, little Arthur," he snarled, "the little hero!"

"Don't be silly, Hector," she laughed.

"Arthur a hero!"

His rising wrath moderated. Evidently what he had said to her had done some good. Still suspicious, and with a horrid sense of unreality, he slipped his arm about her waist and led her to the couch. It was all unreal and unexpected, he thought, as her golden head rested on his shoulder.

"It's a. long time since we did this," he said. "It reminds me of the raid nights."

She straightened herself up.

"The what nights?"

"The raid nights."

She laughed. Hector in the full ardour of that period which was neither youth nor middle-age, had been a tempestuous lover.

"Dear, you use such queer expressions!"

"Do you remember the siren?" he asked, after a pause, and her head nodded vigorously.

"Yes, the cat—but I got you away from her."

"And how we used to go down into the cellar?" he mused. It seemed a thousand years ago. She straightened up. It was she who was suspicion.

"We never did," she protested. "Really, Hector! I hope you're not thinking of somebody else?"

Before he could answer Jane came in, and Jane, curiously enough, looked much younger.

"Will there be three to dinner, madam?" asked the maid.

Mary nodded.

"Who is the third?" demanded Mr. Smith.

"Oh, no one," said his wife, airily. "I asked Arthur to stay."

He sprang to his feet.

"Arthur! Confound the fellow, hasn't he gone? I won't have him. Do you understand. Marv. I-won't-have-him!"

Again the look of blank astonishment on her face.

"But why not?"

"He's such a nice little gentleman, sir," pleaded Jane. "He sat on my knee and told me such funny stories."

Hector glared from the maid to his wife.

"There you are!" he said, triumphantly. "That's the sort of fellow he is! Sits on her knee and tells her funny stories!"

To his amazement she laughed.

"It's not worth while getting angry—he can dine in the kitchen."

"In the kitchen!"

"Of course, he doesn't care," Mary went on, calmly, "so long as he goes to the White City."

"With whom?"

"Well, I'll take him," said Mary, indifferently. "I rather like the Roly-Poly and the Wiggle-Wag."

With a mighty effort Mr. Smith controlled himself.

"You can't go to the White City. It's been requisitioned by the Government four years ago," he said. "The White City is closed, I tell you. It's where the C3 men get their A1 gratuity—everybody knows that."

There was a strained silence, during which Jane tip-toed from the room.

Hector saw something in his wife's eyes that looked like fear, and failed to diagnose its cause.

"I'm sorry I lost my temper," he said, penitently; "the fact is I'm jealous."

The fear was replaced by a gleam of interest.

"Jealous? Of whom?"

He made a little gesture to cover his discomfort.

"Of you—and Arthur."

"But you're mad," she gasped; "at his age—"

"At his age." said Mr. Smith, icily, "I had been thrown out of the Empire twice."

He did not explain the degree of worldliness which this experience implied, but he left her to gather that it represented a particularly lurid form of precocity.

"I don't understand you to-night," she said, shaking her head.

"I don't understand myself," said Mr. Smith, rising. "I think I'll run down to the club, I promised to meet an ace."

"An ace? I thought you'd given up cards."

"You don't understand me—this fellow brought down thirty."

"Thirty what?"

"Boche."

"It isn't 'bosh'!" she exploded. "How did he bring them down?"

Hector groaned.

"He got on their tails and crashed them," he explained, patiently.

She was shocked.

"Poor things! I suppose they broke quite easily?" she asked.

He looked at her.

"I don't know what you are talking about," he said, irritably. "I am speaking about a fellow who has been 'mentioned' six times."

She shook her head.

"This is the first time you have mentioned him to me," she said; "what has he done?"

"Done? Why, in the early days before he started flipping, he took a pill-box all by himself!"

Her mouth opened.

"A whole box?" she gasped.

"You see," he explained, "he was in a tank, and when they went over the top—"

"Over the top of the tank?" she asked, hazily.

"No, the tank went over the top and a minnie dropped in front of him."

She was interested again.

"Poor girl," she said, sympathetically, "and did he help her up?"

"No; you see, a dying pig burst just behind him."

"But what did he do with Minnie?" she demanded.

She could not grapple with pigs that flew, but Minnie was someone tangible.

"Oh, she got him in the leg," he stated, carelessly.

She was grave now.

"I see, she wasn't a lady?"

"Of course she wasn't a lady," he wailed.

"I have told you it wasn't a lady! It was a minenwerfer."

She did not want to hear about Miss Werfer or even of a low person to whom he made glib reference—a Miss Emma Gee. This friend of her husband's seemed to have low tastes. He crashed people, he got on their tails.

"And Big Bertha—" Hector was saying when she stopped him.

"I don't think I want to meet your friend," she said, and made for the door.

He didn't understand her. Usually she was as full of the jargon of the war as the most ardent subaltern. Now she professed ignorance and demanded an elucidation of the most commonplace phrase.

He was pondering on this fact when the maid came into the room. She stood nervously waiting, and Hector guessed her errand.

"Well?" he growled.

"I-I thought I would ask you, sir," she faltered; "I was going to ask the mistress if-if she would give me a little rise."

"A rise again!" he groaned. This was the third or was it the fourth time...?

"But, sir?"

"Now listen to me," he said, severely, "I know that living is expensive, and coals are dear, and I am willing to give you another rise. But this must be the very last time. You can have five pounds a month, but not a penny more."

She did not swoon. She was too well-bred a servant.

"Five pounds a month! Oh, thank you, master, thank you! Oh, you are most good—" she grew incoherent.

Hector raised his eyebrows. He thought she was unusually grateful. His wife returned at that moment to hear his news.

"By the way, dear, I've just raised Jane's wages."

Usually she objected to his interfering in her domestic affairs, but now she was most amiable.

"I promised her I would—she seems a nice girl."

"Yes," said Hector. "I'm giving her five pounds a month."

His wife grasped a chair for support.

"Are you mad?" She beckoned Jane, for her earlier suspicions were now certainties.

"Fetch a doctor," she said, under her breath. "The master isn't well. I only pay her eighteen pounds a year."

She tried to say this in a light conversational tone, but her voice shook.

"You only—?" Something was very wrong, and he called the maid to him. "Ask Dr. Sawyer to step round. Mrs. Smith isn't quite herself," he said.

"Get Dr. Thomas." demanded Mary, sharply.

Thomas! Thomas was in Mesopotamia! It was clear now. The worry of the past years had turned her brain. It was a flattering explanation for the preference she had lately shown to Arthur. They watched one another apprehensively after the girl had gone, then:—

"Feel better, ducky?" he asked, huskily.

"Has that nasty wuzzy feeling gone, lovey?" her voice was a nervous squeak.

Dr. Thomas had the flat opposite, and Dr. Thomas was coming out of his flat when the frightened maid had literally flung herself upon him.

"They're both mad," she babbled, and the startled doctor followed her to where two people, each standing at the extreme end of a long drawing-room, were watching one another in silence. Hector saw him and uttered an exclamation of astonishment.

"By Jove. I thought you were in Bagdad?"

The doctor laid his soothing hand on the other's shoulder.

"Of course—Bagdad! Ah, that's the place—we'll soon put you right, old man."

Ignoring the implication that he wasn't right, Mr. Smith whispered something in the other's ear.

"Of course she is," replied Thomas, indulgently, and caught Mary's eye and Mary's significant signal.

It was at that moment that Arthur came in—Arthur in his Eton suit, with his cherubic face stained with jam. Hector looked at him and his jaw dropped.

"What the devil have you dressed like this for?" he demanded.

"Because I'm going to school, Mr. Smith."

"To school? How old are you?"

"Fourteen—nearly."

"Fourteen!" repeated Hector, hollowly.

"Is it possible—?"

On Mary's desk was a calendar and to this he walked.

"Nineteen fourteen! Mary, I understand all. I will explain. You're not mad—it was the fairy—who put back the clock!—my wish was granted!"

The doctor looked at Mary and Mary looked at the doctor. "I'm going to prophesy," Hector went on, excitedly. "We are going to war! The Kaiser will abdicate! The British Army will be seven millions strong! We shall win the war, thanks to Beatty, Haig, and Foch!"

He saw the round face of Arthur and—smack! Arthur sprawled on the door, blubbering.

"Why did you do that?" asked the terrified Mary.

"He's going to cause me a lot of trouble," said Hector, prophetically.

The Death Room

'DO you believe in spiritualism, Mr Gillette?'

Detective-Inspector John Gillette now frowned a little terrifyingly at the girl who sat on the opposite side of his desk. When an official of Scotland Yard receives a newspaper reporter he does not expect to be cross-examined on his hobbies. And spiritualism was a hobby of this dour man.

'You see,' Ella Martin broke in eagerly, 'I have taken up a case for the paper. The editor did not like the idea at all, and said that my job was to write nice, chatty little pars about what Lady So-and-So wore at the Devonshire House ball, and all that sort of thing, but I rather insisted.'

John Gillette concealed a smile—and he very seldom felt the inclination to smile. She was very young and very pretty, and very unlike any newspaper reporter he had ever seen.

'How did you know I was interested in spooks?' he asked.

'From the evidence you gave in the Marriot case years and years ago. It was amongst the cuttings in the library.'

Detective-Inspector John Gillette was not an easy man to interview. Against that, however, was the fact that very few, other than those officials at police headquarters whose business brought them in touch with him, regarded him as worth interviewing. His name rarely appeared in print, for he was an 'office man' and a consultant rather than a practitioner in the art of crime detection.

He was a man of thirty, and a bachelor in a double sense of the word, for he held a degree from the London University.

'Spiritualism?' he repeated slowly, 'Well, yes and no. Certain phenomena are inexplicable. Animal instinct, for example. I have seen sheep terrified before the door of a new slaughter-house, and one that has never been used before. I have known dogs to be frantic with fear hours before an earthquake. In fact, I have seen my old terrier shivering with fright three hours before a raid warning was received. Explain that! It is as easy to explain as spirit manifestations. There is a something. The mediums feel it, and, dissatisfied with its faint message, they must interpret the whisper as a shout! They see things dimly, and in their impatience or enthusiasm they insist that you shall see plainly. With this result—that they fake. They rip along ahead of the thing they should pursue, and are mad with you when you prove that all that is following them is their own silly shadows! But why are you so interested? It doesn't seem a very healthy subject for a young lady to discuss with a police officer! What is the stunt behind your question?'

She smiled.

'Have you ever heard of Mr Jean Bonnet?' she asked.

The Vampire of Wembley

The inspector's forehead puckered.

'Bonnet! Do you mean the stockbroker?'

She nodded.

'That is the gentleman. He is a millionaire, and has a big, rambling place, Tatton Corners, near Reading.'

Gillette pushed himself back from the table and frowned again.

'A Russian died there the other day. I remember! So that is your stunt? What were the circumstances of the death? All the details were not in the newspapers, and I wasn't very much interested.'

'So I gather,' said the girl, with a little smile. 'Otherwise you would not ask why I want to know something about spiritualism. The Russian's name was Dimitri Nicoli, a financier, who was associated with Mr Bonnet. Nicoli, who lived in Paris, seems to have been a furtive, secretive man. He had no relations and very few friends, certainly nobody who enjoyed his confidence. He had a leaning towards the shadier side of finance, and undoubtedly during the War he dabbled in one or two questionable enterprises which yielded him a huge profit. About four weeks ago Nicoli came to London, and to a man who knew him and who remembered him in town, he confided the fact that he was engaged in a transaction with Mr. Bonnet which would yield him "milliards." The character of the transaction he never discussed, and the next day he left for Tatton Corners, where he arrived and was entertained by Mr Bonnet. He spent a week there, talking over some business. Mr Bonnet says it was the flotation of a culture pearl company on an extensive scale; at any rate, Nicoli left at the end of the week for Paris.

'He returned in the early part of last week, and, at his own request, was put in what the servants at Tatton Corners call "the haunted room".'

'The haunted room?' repeated Gillette. 'Of course! I remember now. There was a headline about it in your newspaper.'

She nodded.

'Apparently one of the rooms—and, curiously enough, it is one of the newest rooms in the most modern wing of the house—is believed to be haunted. Mr Bonnet, who studies spiritualism, and who, like so many people who take up the study, is a hard-headed business man'—she shot a swift glance at Gillette, and for the second time he smiled—'told our reporter that he has seen dark shapes come and go down the corridor, and even through the closed door of the room. He has never mentioned the fact before for fear of frightening the servants.

'The morning after Nicoli's return he was found dead in his bed, and had the appearance of a man who had been strangled, though there were no marks at all upon his body. Suspicion immediately fell upon a mysterious Frenchman, or, at any rate, a man of foreign appearance, who had arrived in the neighbourhood at the same time as Nicoli, and who stayed at the little inn in the village and spent his nights wandering about the country, and was seen by Mr Bonnet's gardener in the grounds of Tatton Corners itself.'

John Gillette tapped the table impatiently.

'You will think we are asleep at Scotland Yard, but I had forgotten all about it! I remember now. But the local police were perfectly satisfied that nothing was wrong. Could this foreigner have reached Nicoli through the window?'

She shook her head.

'I have seen the plans of the house. That wing is newly built, and it is almost impossible for anybody to have got into the room without leaving some trace.'

'And the mysterious Frenchman?'

'Has disappeared entirely. He gave the name of Binot. And now comes the remarkable part of the story. Mr Bonnet sent for one of our reporters yesterday and told him that he had had a communication with the dead man, who had appeared to him that night by the side of his bed with the news that Binot was the murderer!'

'H'm!' growled the detective, settling back in his chair. 'That sounds to me like a disordered digestive apparatus, aggravated by an attack of nerves. I shouldn't take that too seriously if I were you, Miss Martin. Your editor, now—was he interested?'

'Not very,' said the girl; 'but it occurred to me that there might be a bigger story behind it all.'

The Vampire of Wembley

Detective-Inspector John Gillette was silent for a while, absorbed in his own thoughts.

'I should like to see this haunted room,' he said at length, and her eyes lit up.

'I hoped you would,' she said. 'You see, Mr Gillette, I am not frantically impressed by the spirit theory; whilst I can't help feeling that there is something just a little uncanny, I am certain that there is also something scientific behind it too. And science rattles me.'

The detective looked at the eager face and his heart went out to the girl. There was something very naive and appealing in her youth, something that stirred a chord in his nature that had never been touched before.

'Briefly, what is the stunt?' he asked, and she hesitated.

'I was going to do it myself, and then I got a little frightened and realized that detective work isn't as easy as it seems. I thought I would go to Tatton Corners, pretending that I was a fellow countryman of Mr Nicoli—a niece who was interested in his fate. They say Mr Bonnet is awfully kind and unsuspicious.' She hesitated again.

'And when you have taken advantage of his innocence and secured an entry to his house, what then?' asked Gillette, with a twinkle in his eyes.

She pulled a little face.

'I don't know,' she said vaguely. 'Probably get permission to sleep in the haunted room.'

It was Inspector Gillette who hesitated now. He really was not interested in a newspaper mystery which was probably no mystery at all, but he was very much interested in Ella Martin.

'I hate helping the Press,' he said, 'but I'll go with you, though I've an uncomfortable feeling that I'm being a fool. Of course, nobody will invite you to stay, and probably I shouldn't let you if they did. It's a mad adventure, and I look like being turned out of the Force for helping you!'

II

A BITTERLY cold wind was blowing, and there was a smell of snow in the air when they arrived at Tatton Corners. In their assumed character of Russians they were wearing fur coats and hats.

Mr Bonnet, a slight, sad-looking man, was playing patience in his drawing-room when the station fly clattered up the drive. The thin, almost aesthetic-looking face of the financier, the high forehead and the straight grey eyebrows, held the detective's attention. It was the face of a dreamer, of the spiritualist rather than one who had been the shrewdest financier in the country.

Mr Bonnet listened in sympathetic silence whilst the girl (with a glibness which amazed the detective) explained the object of the visit.

'A relation?' asked Mr Bonnet gravely, and she nodded. 'I would, of course, do anything for a relative of my poor friend Nicoli,' said Mr Bonnet with a little sigh, 'though it saddens me even to discuss the tragedy. Perhaps Mr—' He looked at the inspector inquiringly.

'Gillette,' said that gentleman, and Mr Bonnet bowed.

'I had a fear at first that you were reporters, although I am hardened to that now,' said the financier, as he led the way out of the room into the chill of the garden. 'I seem to have lived in the company of policemen and newspaper reporters all my life. Here is the room.'

Tatton Corners was a sixteenth-century farmhouse, to which its owner had made certain ruthless additions, none of which was calculated to improve it from the point of view of the artist. The new wing was of red brick, and some half-hearted attempt had been made to keep the annexe in harmony with the remainder of the structure.

Gillette looked up. A broad window, the top sash of which had been dropped down a foot, a window box, and—

'What is that red square underneath the window?' he asked.

'That is a ventilator,' replied Mr Bonnet. 'I had the new wing built on the soundest hygienic principles, and I fixed these patent ventilators in every room. There is another, you will notice.' He pointed to a window.

He led them round the grounds, which must have been beautiful in summer, and all the time Gillette's eyes did not seem to leave the house.

The Vampire of Wembley

'You are utilitarian at the cost of good architecture,' he laughed. He pointed to a large red tank which the girl had mistaken for a turret structure.

'I hoped nobody would ever notice that,' said the melancholy Mr Bonnet. 'The water supply here isn't sufficient, and we are inclined to dry up during the summer. So I store my rainwater, and at that height we can get sufficient pressure to reach the farthest part of the grounds.'

They passed into the house, and Mr Bonnet led the way to the haunted room. It lay at the end of a passage, from which opened two other doors, leading, as the host showed them, to spare bedrooms. The door was unlocked, and Bonnet flung it open wide.

The detective saw a very ordinary bedroom, comfortably furnished. Beside the bed in the corner there was a dressing-table, a writing-desk, two or three chairs and a small but handsome Persian rug upon the polished floor.

'There, you see, is the other side of the ventilator.' Mr Bonnet pointed to the grille in the wall. 'It is a curious thing that this room should be haunted, because it has rather haunted me.' He smiled pathetically. 'I intended this to be my own sitting-room, but somehow I could never work in it. I experimented with every kind of lighting.' He pointed to the electrolier fastened to the ceiling (a little too rich, the girl thought, for so commonplace a room). 'First I tried lighting it from the walls, and then from the roof; then I tried hand lamps, but somehow I could never settle down to work here, and so I turned it into a spare bedroom. The view sometimes tempts me to come up, or used to tempt me'—he shivered—'until this hideous tragedy got rid of any desire I had to spend my afternoons here.'

Absent-mindedly John Gillette fingered the silver electric switches near the door. Suddenly the light blazed in the roof. He turned another switch, but there was no further illumination.

'The wall lamp is out of order. I am going to have it wired,' said Mr Bonnet. 'I feel I don't wish to do anything to this room now that my poor friend—' He turned away his head.

Ella Martin found herself ushered into the passage and into the hall, and felt for a moment desperate. She had come determined to stay the night, but

116

the absence of women servants, no less than the failure of her host to issue an invitation, made the plan look just a little mad—as mad as Gillette thought it was.

Mr Bonnet accompanied them to the waiting fly.

'I was hoping,' he said, 'that you good people would have stayed the night. But I am very lonely here; half my servants have left, and the new ones are already terror-stricken.'

The detective, with one foot on the step, turned and looked at Ella thoughtfully.

'It would be no great hardship, staying a night in this lovely house. And the hotel doesn't seem to be a very inviting one. Perhaps we can lay the ghost.'

Ella hesitated. For a moment her courage forsook her. The adventure had lost a little of its attractiveness. A glimpse of Gillette's face decided her.

'I'll send the driver back to the hotel to bring a suit-case,' said Gillette. 'I'm glad you asked me. I would rather like to stay here. By the way, are you making a rockery garden, Mr Bonnet?'

'Yes,' said the other in surprise. 'Why?'

'I saw a heap of broken marble at the back of the house,' said the detective. 'But why rockery gardens should not have gravel under foot, and must have unpleasantly sharpened, pointed marble pebbles, heaven only knows!'

They talked of gardens and gardening, and the evening passed so quickly that the girl was surprised to discover it was eleven o'clock.

'I am afraid you will have to be accommodated in the haunted wing,' said Mr Bonnet, smiling for the first time. 'I hope your nerves are good.'

'Excellent,' said the detective. 'I undertake to lay any ghost I find.'

The other became instantly grave.

'I don't think I should speak slightingly of these things, if I were you, Mr Gillette,' he said. 'I am only a child in the science, but I have seen amazing things happen.' He seemed to stop himself with an effort, as though he were afraid of placing too great a strain upon their credulity.

'And the young lady?' He looked at the girl dubiously.

'The young lady...' Ella found her breath coming more quickly; she had to force the words.

'The young lady would like to sleep in the haunted room itself,' she said a little unsteadily, and Mr Bonnet stared at her.

'In the haunted room?' he gasped. 'Impossible, my dear young friend! Why, you would be frightened.'

He looked appealingly at Gillette, and then beckoned him aside.

'I do not know, sir, in what relationship you stand with this young woman,' he said in a low voice, 'but I beg that you persuade her to change her mind.'

An hour before the detective would have been in a dilemma. Now, however, his mind was very clear on all matters except Miss Ella Martin.

'I think I should allow the young lady to sleep where she wishes,' he said calmly, and Mr Bonnet was obviously nonplussed.

'Very good,' he said with a shrug. 'But I must prepare the room—no servant will go into it after dark.'

For a moment the girl's resolution wavered, but her host was gone before she could change her mind.

'I'm scared to death,' she said in a low voice.

'Don't be,' said Gillette, and tapped three times on the table.

'You hear that?—remember it, and when you hear that sound on your bedroom door open and let me in. You'll stay up all night, of course?'

'But—' she began, bewildered.

'You wanted an adventure,' he said grimly, 'and you wanted ghosts. You have bewitched a respectable police officer into acting the fool to that end, and I rather fancy that—'

He had heard Mr Bonnet's footsteps in the room above the library where they were talking, and then:

'Whoo-oo-oo!'

It was a moan that rose to a wail, and then to a shrill shriek ... and silence.

And at that moment Mr Bonnet came slowly down the stairs towards them.

It was Gillette who asked the question.

Mr Bonnet shook his head.

'I don't know,' he said simply. 'I hear it often—it is the sound which frightens the servants. Your room is ready, Miss Nicoli,' he said, using the name she had given. And with reluctant feet she walked upstairs.

The bed had been made and she sat down, looking fearfully about the room. It was nearly twelve o'clock before a tap brought her heart to her mouth, and she opened the door to admit the detective. He seemed to be amused at something as he turned and locked the door. He carried a bag in his hand, and this he opened and took out a small black cardboard box. From this he extracted two tin candlesticks, into which he fitted two short candle lengths.

'Are you preparing for the lights to go out?' she said in a whisper.

'Not exactly. I am preparing for their coming on,' said the other. 'Will you oblige me by sitting bolt upright, Miss Martin. Sit on a pillow and keep very, very quiet, because this ghost hates noise.'

He walked to the window and tried to open the lower sash, but it had been fastened, and he remembered Mr Bonnet apprising him of the fact. The top sash, however, he pulled down.

'Not that it will be much use,' he said.

He took off the silken shade from the wall bracket.

'Why, there is no electric bulb in it,' said the girl in surprise. 'That is why it doesn't light.'

'I didn't think there would be,' said the other, replacing the silk shade.

Pulling down the blind he lit the two candles and placed them on the floor; then he switched out the light.

'Watch the candles,' he whispered.

III

THE girl sat, watching and watching, until there seemed a dozen dancing candles, until her very head ached from weariness. No sound broke the stillness of the night; the faint roar and rattle of distant trains came to them at intervals, but there was no other sound. Once Gillette turned his head and looked at the wall bracket, but that was the only movement he made, and then, for no reason whatever, one of the candles went out.

The Vampire of Wembley

The girl stared at the remaining light. Whilst she looked that too went out. 'Don't move!' hissed Gillette.

Suddenly there was the flash of an electric torch.

'Hold that,' he whispered. He took a box of matches out of his pocket, lit one, steadied it until the flame had taken hold and then slowly lowered the light toward the candle. An inch from the top of the wick the light went out.

'Take off your shoes,' whispered the detective, and switched on the lights. 'No, no, don't stoop, put your feet up on the bed. That's right.'

Tiptoeing to the door he turned the key softly and pushed. The door did not give by so much as a millimetre. She saw the frown gather on his face as he turned the handle.

'The ghost has bolted us in,' he said nonchalantly. 'I was a fool not to look for bolts.'

He lit the candles again and slowly lowered one to the floor. It went out just below the bed level.

'I always carry candles in my kit,' he said conversationally. 'I wish I carried an axe.'

He went to the window and examined the panes.

'Toughened glass strengthened by wire,' he said. 'We must have time.'

She saw him glance up at the wall bracket, and then, kneeling on the bed, he screwed up a piece of paper and leisurely plugged the open end of the fixture.

Over the open window sash he vaulted, lowering himself to the ledge without.

'Come here and bring your scarf,' he ordered, and, wondering, she obeyed. 'Hold up one hand.'

In an instant he had knotted an end of the scarf about her wrist, and drew up the slack until the strain on her arm was almost painful. Then he fastened the other end to the hinge of the outside shutter.

'What are you doing?' she gasped.

'Women faint,' said Mr Gillette coolly, 'and I particularly wish you not to faint until I return.'

A second later he disappeared.

Her wrist pained her; the agony was almost as much as she could bear, and she seemed in danger of fulfilling his prophecy when she heard the rasp of wood against the window ledge and he appeared.

'A ladder,' he said, and helped her over the open sash.

She saw nothing, but he guided her to the ladder's head.

How she got down she could never remember. She was trembling in every limb when at last she reached the ground. Still she could see nothing. The night was pitch black. Large, wet snowflakes brushed against her cheek, and an icy wind swept through the tree-tops, filling the night with a dismal sound, and chilled her to the bone despite her heavy fur coat.

'I'm afraid I shall have to carry the ladder, but in a little while your eyes will get used to the darkness,' he said, 'and you will see ahead.'

He shouldered the ladder, and she followed blindly. No light showed in the house, but presently they came to a corner which was, she remembered, the corner where first she had seen the red tank.

'Will you stay here or come with me?' he asked in a low voice.

'Where are you going?' she whispered fearfully.

'Looking for ghosts,' was the grim reply, and then she laughed a little hysterically.

'I think I had better see them too,' she said.

He was planting the ladder against a wall unbroken by windows. Presently she heard the grate of his feet on the rungs. Biting her trembling lip she gripped the sides of the ladder and began to climb. Half-way up an attack of vertigo almost brought her down, and the man above her must have been possessed of supernatural senses, for, even as she swayed, he caught her.

'A little farther,' he whispered, and with his aid she scrambled to the top.

She could see now clearly; she was on a flat leaded roof.

'Take off your shoes,' he whispered, and she obeyed.

They crept forward to the very middle of the oblong patch, and there she discerned something which looked like a small platform raised a few inches above the roof level.

The Vampire of Wembley

'This may not be the place at all,' he whispered in her ear, 'but I've been drawing a mental plan of the house, and I imagine my guess is right.'

Stooping, he gripped the edge of the platform and drew it up an inch. No light showed, and, peering down, he saw that the trap covered a glass fanlight. Cautiously he lifted the trap still farther and laid it back, the girl at his side. Then from the room below came a sudden brilliant flash of light, and they looked down speechless, for in that flash was revealed the hideous paraphernalia of destruction.

The room was long and narrow, lined with white-glazed brick. In the centre was a large retort, near which was a heap of those marble chips that they had seen in the garden that afternoon. Attached to a pipe leading from the retort was a small electric pump which worked ceaselessly.

The girl could only stare in amazement. The significance of the retort and the working pump did not come to her. Her eyes were fixed upon a bearded man who lay, strapped to a narrow table, gagged and helpless.

'Binot!' she gasped.

The detective gripped her arm so fiercely that she winced. His eyes were on Bonnet, who stood in his shirt-sleeves, his hands thrust in his pockets, a smile of sardonic amusement upon his face, as he caught the glaring eyes of the prisoner on the table.

He was saying something, but the sound did not penetrate through the glass, or rise above the moan of the wind.

Gillette stooped and felt desperately for the edge of the fanlight. To his surprise it was not locked, but came up in his hands, and the queer, sickening odour of the room struck him in the face and made him choke.

'My friend,' Bonnet was saying in French, 'I suffer from a plague of detectives. First there was you, whom our admirable friend Nicoli brought to Tatton Corners because he feared, very rightly, that I would steal the eight million francs he brought with him. And you, I admit, were difficult! Then we have the admirable Detective-Inspector Gillette, accompanied by a girl who has a cock-and-bull story of being a relative of Nicoli.'

He laughed softly, and took up the long knife that lay upon a table near the bench and felt the edge with his finger. Then he laughed again.

'Our Gillette is dead by now,' he said calmly. 'I watched him join his young lady, and it is better to be dead than compromised. The beauty of it is that nobody will ever discover—'

He walked across to where the glaring Frenchman lay, and tried his knife again ...

Gillette flung open the fanlight and leapt upon the madman.

IV

'BEFORE I came upon this perilous adventure I looked up Mr Bonnet in an old work of reference, and I found that his hobby was chemistry,' said Inspector Gillette, as they were travelling back to town, 'and when I discovered that the electric wall lamp was fixed on the end of a hollow pipe I began to wonder where the pipe led to. Obviously in building the wing, and for this especial room, Bonnet connected the wall bracket with a hollow pipe which led to his laboratory. Bonnet must have planned the murder some time ago; he had been in correspondence with Nicoli, an old confederate of his, for more than a year. That is to say, before the builders put trowel to brick on the new annexe.

'By some means which we may discover, but very likely shall never know, he persuaded Nicoli to bring an enormous sum of money to London, and the bait must have been a fairly golden one. Nicoli mistrusted his former friend, or else had no desire to travel with so much money without an escort, and he engaged Binot to follow him and watch him. When Binot found his master was dead, and there was no mention of the money, instead of getting back and reporting to Paris to the French authorities he decided to wait and investigate independently. I am not imputing any motive to Binot,' said Gillette, shaking his head, 'but human nature being what it is, I should imagine Binot wanted to get the money that his master had. He came, was captured, and he has been a prisoner for a month.

'To-night Bonnet decided to kill three birds with one stone. I am not sure,' said Gillette thoughtfully, 'whether it was just carbonic acid gas, or whether it was carbon monoxide. They are both very heavy gasses. They are both odourless, tasteless, and they could both be poured into a room while a man was sleeping or sitting.'

'But the moaning ghost?' asked the girl.

Gillette chuckled.

'The moaning ghost put me on to it. Obviously it was an electric fan placed behind the ventilator and operated from Bonnet's room. He turned a switch and the fan began to revolve. He touched a switch and it stopped. The fan, of course, was to clear the room of the gas, so that any person coming in afterwards would not detect the slightest trace of it. The other ventilators were fakes. The death room was designed for Nicoli and his millions—how many millions we may never know.

'Last night I had a talk with Bonnet, and dropped a hint that I knew his game, without exactly intimating that I understood the method he adopted. I did mention the fact that a fairly deadly gas can be made from marble chips treated with hydrochloric acid, and I guess that hit home, for he is sane enough to be annoyed by the ease with which he was bowled over. There would have been a sad accident last night, my young friend, if you had gone to sleep in that room without the warning candle—nothing burns in either carbonic acid or carbon monoxide—and without the knowledge that our dear friend was spending the night profitably in generating the real spirit of the death room.

'I hope I shall see you again,' said Gillette at parting, and held her hand. 'I can't promise you ghosts, and I won't advise you to look round the Black Museum. Do you ever write stories?'

'Sometimes,' she smiled.

'Tell me, is it a convention of literature that a girl marries the man who rescues her from—er—death and all that sort of thing?'

She went very red, but did not take her eyes from his.

'It is a convention—in detective stories,' she said.

Which seemed to Gillette, in the circumstances, a completely satisfactory answer.

Edgar Wallace

The Sodium Lines

MR HERBERT FALLOWILL made his final entry on a square card almost covered with his neat and microscopic writing, took up the dead end of his cigar from the edge of the ash-tray and lit it. He was a square-built man, clean-shaven, except for a fiery moustache, and his reddish hair ran back from a forehead that was high and bald.

'You leave for Queenstown to-night?' he said, and the thin-lipped woman who bore his name nodded.

'The passports?'

'Yours is in the name of "Clancy",' he said. 'Mine is fixed. I shall leave as arranged by the Aquitania. You'll meet me at the apartment on 44th Street—I shall be there at eleven-fifteen. This is the time-table—'

He fixed a pair of pince-nez on his thick nose and consulted the card.

'At nine o'clock Dorford will give me the cheque; at nine- thirty it will be cashed, and I shall move to Southampton—quick! I have relay cars waiting at Guildford and Winchester. The Aquitania leaves dock at twelve-thirty—I shall make it, with time to spare. The old man will not expect to see me again on the Saturday or Sunday because I've told him I'm going away. Monday is a holiday and the banks are closed. The earliest he can discover anything is by Tuesday morning.'

She took out the cigarette she was smoking and blew a cloud to the ceiling.

'That old man is certainly dippy!' she said, shaking her head.

Mr Fallowill smiled indulgently.

'There never was a pure scientist that wasn't,' he said. 'Only so very few of 'em have the stuff.'

Professor Dorford had no illusions about himself. Business of all kinds worried him, and he accounted himself fortunate that, after a succession of incompetents, heaven had sent him a most capable middle-aged secretary, who combined an exceptional knowledge of finance with a capacity for knowing just what the Professor would say in answer to people who pester a rich man with requests for subscriptions or charitable assistance.

He would have gone farther and favoured his secretary with a power of attorney which would enable him to draw small cheques for the tradespeople, but here Gwenn Dorford, a nineteen-year-old graduate, put her small foot down very firmly.

'My dear lamb!' she said, and when the Professor was addressed as a dear lamb in that tone of voice, he invariably shivered.

'Fallowill is a most excellent man,' he protested feebly.

'I don't like Mr Fallowill, and I loathe his wife,' said Gwenn, 'but I realize that I may be prejudiced—and, after all, a woman can be a good wife and still be a cat to everybody else. Mr Spooner, the bank manager, says—'

'Spooner is an interfering jackanapes,' said the Professor testily. 'I am seriously thinking of taking my account away from the Gresham Bank. To—er—impugn Fallowill's—er—honour is monstrous! He had letters from eminent people in Australia and the United States.'

Nobody knew better than Gwenn Dorford that her father had not verified these excellent references, but she did not press the matter to an argument.

She did, however, tell Johnny Brest for the fortieth time, and for the fortieth time Johnny sympathised with her. But then, Johnny would. He was tactful, as became an officer in the Public Prosecutor's department and a lawyer at that; he was sympathetic, because—Gwenn was very pretty and he carried her portrait in his cigarette case.

'He may be all right,' he said. 'I went over to New Scotland yard and tried to find out whether anything was known about him—he is quite a stranger to police headquarters.'

'I don't wish him to become acquainted through us,' she said firmly. 'He may be the nicest man in the world, but the way daddy trusts him makes my hair stand up! And now, Johnny, you can take me a long drive in your pot boiler.'

Johnny Brest was the owner of a steam car, because that was the only kind of car he could afford to buy. Not that such machines are cheap. They were certainly rare in England—so rare that, when one was offered for sale by auction, Johnny, who had drifted into the rooms out of curiosity, heard the car offered at so ridiculously low a figure that, in a moment of recklessness, he bid, and found himself the proprietor of a machine that nobody understood. It was only then that he discovered the secret of its propulsion.

Mr Fallowill watched the noiseless white car slip down the drive and disappear from view, as he had watched it scores of times. He felt easier in his mind when the antagonistic daughter of his employer was away from the house, and more especially was he relieved that afternoon.

Returning to his desk, he cleared off his correspondence and went in search of Professor Dorford. The Professor looked up as his secretary entered. He was a grey, bent man with a vague manner and a trick of ignoring the immediate. Fallowill said of him, with truth, that he lived from three days to ten years behind his time, and certainly it was the fact that most days were gone before John Dorford was aware that they had arrived.

'Ah, Fallowill! Come in, come in, please. Will you get on to Sir Roland Field—Cambridge 99 or 999—or perhaps it is some other number—'

'Cambridge 9714,' said the secretary.

'Of course! I was sure you would remember. Will you be so good as to ask him if I am—er—mad in supposing that the sodium lines disappeared from the spectrum this morning? It is an extraordinary fact, my dear Fallowill, that when I was making a very superficial examination of the sun's spectrum, those lines appeared and disappeared, and finally vanished altogether for the space of twelve minutes!'

Fallowill inclined his head and adopted the requisite expression of amazement. The peculiarities of the sun's spectrum meant nothing to him. Inwardly he cursed his employer's dislike of the telephone, for he knew his own limitations, and a scientific discussion on a long-distance wire was beyond him.

'Certainly, sir. Did you think any more about the matter I mentioned to you?'

The Professor scratched his head in perplexity.

'The matter—now what was that, Fallowill?'

'The question of transferring your balance to the Wales and Western bank.'

The Vampire of Wembley

Professor Dorford sighed—he always sighed when money was a subject of discussion.

'Yes, yes, of course, Fallowill. I quite agree, and I shall certainly act on your advice. I will make the transfer—when?'

'Saturday is the end of the month!' suggested Fallowill.

Even Gwenn paid a grudging acknowledgement to Mr Fallowill's financial genius, and justly so. For, in various names and in divers countries, he had so manipulated the finances of confiding investors that it had been necessary from time to time to make startling changes in his appearance. And now he had rendered the Professor an immense service. Foreseeing the industrial slump, he had induced his employer to turn all but his government stock into money.

'Saturday? Yes,' said the Professor. 'When is Saturday?'

'To-morrow,' replied the other. 'Brighton Rails are down to three. We got out of those in time! I was calculating to-day that, if you hadn't started selling when I suggested, you would have been eight thousand to the bad. You can't make a mistake by holding the cash instead. Short term loans pay very little interest, but you have the money to jump into the market when it strikes bottom.'

'Exactly,' murmured Mr Dorford agreeably. 'I'm greatly obliged to you, Fallowill. And now will you get Sir Roland?'

Waiting for the call to come through, the sturdy secretary marshalled his knowledge of the spectrum. He knew that when the rays of the sun passed through a prism it threw bands of variegated light on a screen. He knew that there was a more complicated apparatus which showed in the rainbow hue bright and dark lines which indicated the presence in the sun of certain elements. To keep pace with his employer's requirements, he had struggled through various text-books on the subject, and knew, therefore, that sodium was one of the more important of the solar elements.

It was some time before he got his call through to Sir Roland, and that aged gentleman, who shared his fellow scientist's dislike of the telephone, was in his most irritable mood.

'What's that? Sodium—who wants sodium? Is it Dorford himself? What do you want, my good fellow?'

'The Professor wishes to know if you have observed the absence of sodium lines in the spectrum,' said the patient Fallowill.

'No, I haven't,' snapped the other. 'Nor has he! You've made a mistake. Get back and tell him to write!'

Crash! went the telephone receiver, and Fallowill went back to his employer to report the result of the conversation. Professor Dorford rubbed his chin nervously.

'Perhaps I was wrong,' he said. 'It may have been some trick of eyesight, but certainly the sodium lines disappeared at eleven-sixteen this morning.'

'Remarkable, sir,' said Fallowill politely.

He lived in West Kensington, and travelled home by tube. His mind was so occupied with the possibilities which to-morrow held that, although he read his evening newspaper, he did not comprehend a single word until his eye was held by a headline: 'Extraordinary Traffic Block.' And then the figures '11.15' arrested him.

*

At 11.15 this morning a most extraordinary traffic block occurred in the heart of the City. By an amazing coincidence, three motor-buses stopped of their own accord in the narrowest part of Cheapside, and could not be moved for a quarter of an hour. As it was the rush hour, the street was soon filled with stationary cars. This in itself might not have been remarkable, but the same phenomenon was witnessed in the Strand, on Ludgate Hill and in other parts of the City.

*

He was waiting on the platform for the car to slow into South Kensington Station when the conductor, whom he knew by sight, looked at the paper he was carrying.

'Queer thing, that traffic stoppage,' he said. 'It happened down here.'

'On the tubes?' asked Fallowill in surprise, and the man nodded.

'Yes, we slowed down and all the lights went out. Somebody told me that it was a magnetic storm. I know the telegraph lines weren't working.'

'Queer,' agreed Fallowill, and went home to help his wife pack.

*

GWENN DORFORD did not as a rule see her father before the lunch hour. He was an early riser, and usually closeted himself in his study until midday, and it was a rule of the establishment that he should not be interrupted. She was passing his room an hour before lunch and, seeing the door open, looked in. The Professor was standing at the window, his hands in his pockets, staring moodily into the sunlit street.

'Good morning, daddy. Aren't you working?'

He looked round with a start.

'No, no, my dear,' he said a little nervously. 'I'm—er—not working. I'm going out. Who is that?' He stared past her. 'Oh, it is you, Johnny—Come in, come in. Are you staying to lunch?'

'I'm taking Gwenn to Hampton Court,' said Johnny Brest.

'So you are! Of course, I remember.'

Dorford looked at his watch, and for some remarkable reason the girl felt a little twinge of alarm.

'Where is Mr Fallowill?' she asked.

'Gone to the bank,' said the Professor a little huskily. 'And, Gwenn, the sodium lines are gone again. Remarkable! Sodium has disappeared from the sun!'

'Why has Mr Fallowill gone to the bank?' she asked, not interested for the moment in sodium and its eccentricities.

The Professor looked appealingly to the young man.

'I think I have been rather a fool, Gwenn. It is extraordinary that I should think so, but I do. Though I'm sure Fallowill is as honest as the day, but—'

'What have you done?' she asked quickly.

'I've given him—er—a cheque for eighty-four thousand pounds—he is transferring my account,' said the Professor, and the hand that went up to his mouth was shaking. 'You see, I have a whole lot of fluid capital, and Fallowill thought that it would be better in another bank.'

She gasped.

'You've given him the cheque? But will Mr Spooner pay?'

'I wrote a letter also. Spooner telephoned up to ask if it was all right, and I said yes.'

'To what bank was it to be paid, Mr Dorford?'

'The Wales and Western.'

'We can easily find out,' said Johnny, and took up the telephone. He jerked the hook for a long rime, and then: 'Your phone is out of order.'

'I know.' The Professor nodded. 'I tried to get the bank five minutes ago.'

He was still looking out of the window, his mind apparently concentrated on the fruitless efforts of a chauffeur to start a car on the opposite side of the road.

'That is strange,' he said.

'But, father, why don't you drive round to the bank and ask?'

'I thought of doing that,' he said. 'In fact, I've sent Mary to get a taxi, and here she is.'

A hot and flustered housemaid appeared in the doorway.

'None of the taxis are going, sir,' she gasped.

'Going? What do you mean?'

'The street's full of cabs and cars and they're all standing still! They can't move them, sir. And if you please, sir, none of the telephones are working... a man told me the electric lights have gone too...'

*

WITH a large wad of American bills in his inside pocket, Mr Fallowill moved out of town, exercising that caution which experience had taught him was profitable. An annoyed traffic policeman might make all the difference between the success and failure of his scheme. Once beyond Barnes and out of Kingston, he stepped on the accelerator and the big car roared along the Portsmouth road at sixty miles an hour. Beyond Cobham there was a hill to negotiate, and, reaching the crest, he turned the car at full speed down the steep slope.

And then he heard something and frowned. The engine had stopped, and the car was running downhill under its own weight and impetus. If he had any doubt, it was settled when he came to the foot of the slope. A slight rise a hundred yards along slowed the car, and he had to put on the brakes to prevent the machine from running backwards. Fortunately, there was a wayside inn within a hundred yards, and, after making an ineffectual effort to restart the machine, he walked to the hostel.

To his relief, he saw a telephone wire connecting the house with the main lines.

'I want to telephone to Guildford—' he began.

The landlord shook his head.

'The 'phone is out of order,' he said. 'At least, it was a minute or two ago when I tried to get a call through to Esher.'

Fallowill's heart sank.

'Where is the nearest?' he asked.

'There isn't one within six miles,' said the landlord. 'What is the matter?'

'My car has broken down, and it is absolutely necessary that I should be in Southampton in two hours,' said Fallowill.

He was desperate, but he must risk giving a clue to the police that would lead them eventually to Southampton. Then, to his relief:

'I have an old flivver here that'll run you into Guildford. You will be able to hire a car from there,' said the landlord, and Fallowill could have fallen on his neck. At Guildford the relief car was waiting, thanks to his foresight.

He followed his host out into the yard, where a dilapidated machine stood underneath a shed, and together they pushed the car into the stable yard, whilst a hastily summoned youth struggled into his coat.

'Take this gentleman to Guildford. Where did you leave your machine, sir?'

'At the bottom of the hill.'

'I'll have it brought up,' said the landlord. 'You can call for it on your way back.'

The youth dropped into the driver's seat and Fallowill followed.

'I can't get her to start!' said the surprised chauffeur a few minutes later.

Neither self-starter nor handle had the slightest effect, and after a quarter of an hour Fallowill, white-faced and shaken, stepped to the ground.

*

MANY strange things happened that day. The streets and roads of England were littered with useless motor-cars. Every electric train, above and below ground, had come to a standstill, and from the black tunnels of darkened tube stations poured processions of frightened passengers.

Johnny Brest drove his steam car along Whitehall. The sight was amazing. Motor-cars, motor-buses, great lorries, tiny motor-cycles, stood derelict, and the pavements were crowded with their passengers.

Nowhere was there a telephone or telegraph working, he learnt from the technical expert, who, with the police chiefs, had been summoned to a conference at the Home Office.

And then Johnny saw on his chief's table a big magnet, and wondered who had brought it there.

'Look at this!' said the chief, and, picking up the magnet, held it against a little desk-knife.

'What is the matter?' asked Johnny in perplexity. 'It doesn't seem to be attracting the steel.'

'It has lost its properties, for some extraordinary reason,' said the chief. 'That is why the streets are filled with standing cars. Every piece of metal in the world has become demagnetized!'

For a long time the young man could not grasp the significance of this simple statement.

'We have had electric storms before,' said the technical expert. 'Storms which, for some reason or other, have disorganised telegraphic communication. But this is something worse. Electricity, as created and applied by man for his service, has ceased to exist. Communication throughout the country has practically stopped.'

'But the railways are working.'

The other smiled.

'They are certainly working,' he said drily. 'Trains are being flagged from station to station, and since the telegraph service is out of order, trains will be restricted to two or three a day on the main lines until we can organise some method of signalling by semaphore. There isn't an aeroplane in the sky—the London-Paris service went out of action at ten- forty- five, and we can only hope that the London-Paris machines got down without mishap—there is no means of knowing.'

Later, they were to learn that ships were feeling their way into port, their compasses having ceased to function. Even the gyroscope compass, which depended upon a little electric motor, was valueless under the new and strange conditions.

On the Sunday the Cabinet, which had dispersed for the week- end, reached town, the Premier coming down from Yorkshire by a special train, which took twenty-six hours to do the journey. The Home Secretary, more fortunately placed, came up from Devizes on a steam trolley.

No newspapers appeared on the Sunday—everybody depended upon electric current for its motive power, and the great power works were out of action. Only the streets which were lit by gas had any illumination. On the Monday morning a steam-driven press issued the momentous tidings.

*

The scientists have discovered that an extraordinary revolution is taking place in the sun. The sodium lines have disappeared from the spectrum, and it is an astonishing fact that, for some reason which cannot be understood by the cleverest brains in the world, sodium has been absorbed by some other element, the sun's spectrum revealing amazing chemical changes in the sun's composition. A limited mail service will be carried on by steam tractors, and the Minister of Transport is mobilising all the horses in the country to augment the main railroads, and every effort is being made to secure the food supply. The country must, however, reconcile itself to the possibility that what we know and call electricity, as applied to the service of mankind, may never return to use during the lifetime of the present generation. Fortunately, very few of our collieries are equipped for electric hauling, and all, with the exception of a dozen, are working at full speed to cope with the increased demands of the gas plants.

On the Monday, when the Stock Exchange was opened, scenes of the wildest excitement were witnessed. The oil market suffered the most extraordinary collapse in its history, despite the warnings which were displayed, that all heavy locomotion was practically unaffected by the sun's eccentricity. Rail shares jumped on the rumour that a new method of light signalling had been successfully adopted on the Western region. But the most sensational advance of all was in the gas market. Here stocks soared to undreamt-of prices.

It was humanly impossible to learn what was happening in other parts of the globe. Cable and radio communication were suspended.

*

PROFESSOR DORFORD was a beggar. Before him stretched such a vista as would have reduced an ordinary man to despair, but in the new world problem his own personal misfortune was so insignificant that it was lost to sight.

On the fourth night of the solar disaster, Johnny Brest called to give the latest news.

'Fallowill is still in the country,' he said. 'A car was stranded on the Portsmouth Road, near the Red Lion, on the day the juice went west, and the landlord identified the man—luckily, I stopped at the inn to get water for my magnificent machine—I was offered a thousand pounds for it to-day, by the way.'

'You think he will be found?' asked the girl quickly.

'Certain—he is hiding in the neighbourhood of Guildford. I suppose it will make a big difference to the Professor if the money cannot be recovered?'

She nodded.

'At present he is so absorbed in that wretched sodium that he doesn't realise that he is ruined,' she said. 'Listen!'

From the study came the sound of a booming voice.

'Sir Roland Field,' she said. He came—don't laugh, Johnny—by steam-roller! There are no trains from Cambridge.'

'There is no doubt,' Professor Dorford was saying at that moment with some satisfaction, 'that the only places unaffected by this solar disturbance are the wild villages of Africa.'

'But why sodium?' boomed Sir Roland.

He was an irascible old man, who regarded this phenomenon of nature as a direct affront to himself.

'Why sodium, my good friend? If the iron had gone from the sun, or the magnesium, or any other infernal element, I could understand, but why sodium? What the devil has sodium got to do with electrical energy?'

'I don't know,' admitted Dorford.

'Of course you don't know!' roared the old gentleman. 'It's an absurdity! There isn't a scientist in the world who will not tell you that it is an absurdity! Now, if it were iron or nickel...'

'Is it not possible,' interrupted Professor Dorford, 'that the disappearance of sodium brought about through, let us say, such a chemical conversion as we see every day in our laboratories, may have—'

'No, sir, it isn't possible!' bellowed Sir Roland.

Johnny listened and grinned. He was a busy man. His steam car was one of the most popular means of locomotion in the country. Attached by his chief to the Intelligence Department of the War Office—for the troops were under arms everywhere, guarding the food markets, and augmenting the police, on whom the darkened towns of England threw an additional burden—he had little leisure.

The next day he was on his way to Winchester with despatches to the officer commanding the troops. It was a glorious afternoon, and, peering up at the unclouded brilliance of the sun, he found it hard to believe that that bright friend of the world had played so low a trick upon humanity.

Eight miles from Winchester he saw the gleam of a little river on his right and a huddle of squat factory buildings, and wondered who had laid down an industrial plant in the heart of the smiling countryside. And then he saw a figure walking in the shade of a hedge. It might have been a tramp, so dusty and begrimed was Mr Fallowill, for the fear of detection had kept him to the woods and the hedges.

Edgar Wallace

As he had realised the immense advantages which the failure of the telegraph and mechanical propulsion gave to him, he had grown bolder. No message could warn the police of the towns through which he passed, no swift cars could overtake him. His wife, he guessed, was on the seas and safe; he himself was sufficiently ingenious to devise methods of escape. He touched the pad of crisp papers in his breast pocket and smiled.

And then he heard the soft purr of the steam car and whipped round. As Johnny jumped to the ground, the man turned and, leaping a hedge, ran across the fields toward the little river.

Instantly John Brest was in pursuit. He was younger, more athletic, but the man out-distanced him rapidly. Fallowill reached the river's edge and looked round for some method of crossing. He could not swim, and there was no boat. Hesitating, he looked around. A few hundred yards along the river was some sort of factory building, and, crossing the stream a little way down, was a thick cable supported on either bank by iron trestles.

Darting along the tow-path he gained the first support, climbed, and, catching the cable, went hand over hand across the river.

By the time the pursuer reached the trestle, Fallowill was across. Johnny watched him; saw him reach out his hand to grip the second trestle.

There was no scream, no sound, only a flicker of white light, and Fallowill dropped to the ground a bundle of smoking clothes.

When John Brest, swimming the stream, came up to him, he was dead, and the packet of notes in his pocket was singed brown. For he had crossed by a power cable at the very moment that scientists the world over saw the sodium lines come back to the spectrum of the sun.